red rooms

2007 © Cherie Dimaline

Library and Archives Canada Cataloguing in Publication

Dimaline, Cherie, 1975-

Red rooms / by Cherie Dimaline.

ISBN 978-1-894778-38-1

I. Title.

PS8607.I53R44 2007   C813'.6   C2007-902078-X

Printed in Canada

Printed on Ancient Forest Friendly 100%
recycled post consumer fibre paper

Published by Theytus Books
Edited by Lee Maracle
Copyedited by Sharron Proulx-Turner and Leanne Flett Kruger
Designed by Suzanne Bates
www.theytusbooks.ca

On behalf of Theytus Books, we would like to acknowledge
the support of the following:
We acknowledge the financial support of the Government of
Canada through the Book Publishing Industry Development
Program (BPIDP) for our publishing activities.
We acknowledge the support of the Canada Council for the
Arts which last year invested $20.1 million in writing and
publishing throughout Canada.
Nous remercions de son soutien le Conseil des Arts du
Canada, qui a investi 20,1 millions de dollars l'an dernier
dans les lettres et l'édition à travers le Canada.
We acknowledge the support of the Province of British
Columbia through the British Columbia Arts Council.

  Patrimoine canadien / Canadian Heritage

 Canada Council for the Arts / Conseil des Arts du Canada

 BRITISH COLUMBIA ARTS COUNCIL

red rooms

by: Cherie Dimaline

Theytus Books
Penticton, B.C.

For Edna Dusome (1913-2005)

I did it grandma!

room 414

There is an old saying, 'a servant is a master in disguise'; having the means to make life smooth and also the means to bury comfort and convenience in minute nuisances and tiny fuckups. Servants are genies in scratchy second-hand uniforms granting wishes from their menial bottled accommodations. They are the urban anthropologists, discerning lives and interpreting trends through trash can contents and receipts left on bedside tables. I read once where a cleaning lady turned writer compared herself to Margaret Mead without the finances to get to the South Seas—without the finances or the respect.

The hotel where I work is neither new and fancy nor old and quaint. It's merely a link in a nondescript chain built to feel like any other link in a thousand other cities. It's where people stay when they have moderate expense accounts and very little imagination. There are plastic flowers in the lobby, beige walls in the hallways and hideously shiny, eighties inspired comforters on all the beds. It's not too demanding so as to consume my at-home hours. No one complains if there are streaks on the bathroom mirrors. No one expects mints on 500 count Egyptian cotton pillowcases. I am caught up in the tribal movements of the staff, intrigued by the remains of so many foreign guests. I read their lives through old magazines in bathrooms and piles of change left on bureaus.

1

Located anywhere else, this hotel would be boring. I would be steal-ing drinks from mini bars and sneaking into the hot tub after hours for amusement. But in this city, it becomes a magnifying glass for the human circus that whirls around us twenty four hours a day. Last summer I sat on one of the flat rocks out front of the hotel, smoking the rest of my cigarette before the night shift started. Someone pulled the fire alarm and within minutes the building threw up its entire registry. It was a veritable social autopsy and I sat, like a coroner, reviewing the contents of its appetite, looking for clues as to how it lived and grew.

An old woman in a blue velour robe came first. She carried a walk-er under her arm and was hauling ass out the automatic doors. Behind her was a boy in a little league baseball uniform from 'Al's Garden Centre, Route #54, Bangor, Maine'. He carried a vase of bright red carnations instead of a mitt. Then there were the Black teenage twins who held each other's hands as they ran past the boy and the old lady, all the while yelping nervously. Their nails were easily three inches long and were painted with tiny American flags and fireworks accented with sparkles.

Several versions of the standard businessman poured out like marbles from a spilt sack. They all resembled each other, but upon closer in-spection they had different coloured pinstripes and weights. Each one managed to chat on cell phone headsets, postponing meetings, rescheduling appointments and carrying their all-important brief-cases; even the one who had forgotten to pull on his pants before running out had a cell phone and briefcase.

A young woman wearing a shawl that looked like a navy blue spiderweb walked out slowly. Her face was puffy from tears, her hair knotted from sex. Then a woman with a Chihuahua tucked under one arm and a stack of gowns under the other, arrived. A man with the most unattractive comb-over I had ever seen made his way out the door in the midst of an asthma attack. His cheeks were almost purple in his effort to draw breath. It made me reassess the way I looked at this mediocre collection of rooms in the middle of this huge city. I started paying more attention and stopped hiding out in the laundry room so much.

I would not describe myself as a friendly person. It's an assessment that is supported by the fact that I do not have very many friends. I don't really make an effort to reach out to others. At work, I put on my ear buds and let the music from my MP3 player become the soundtrack to my days. I am in a Fellini movie. I am the interesting and tragic beauty that moves along the plot.

I clean rooms in a hotel and enjoy the gritty repetitiveness combined with the ever changing cast of characters. I get to knock on doors and call out, 'Housekeeping'. Technically I don't have to do this, but since it's what every cleaning lady does in Hollywood, I consider it both my duty and my right. Without these little amusements, the tedium of the work would make me crazy. So, while I fold up comforters and vacuum the same floors over and over again, I listen in on phone calls, read scraps of paper, watch the patrons and fill in the blanks.

The game goes something like this: I find a single black shoe under the bed and a plastic hospital ID bracelet snipped off and thrown in the trash can. From these pieces I imagine that the tall redheaded man who stayed here had recently travelled from a remote Russian village in order to get the surgery he needed for his bum leg. Imagine his horror when he wakes from the procedure and learns that he has been in a coma for a little under a month, having picked up a nasty post-op infection. Worse, his leg has been removed below the knee. He calls his wife back home and tells her that he is leaving her for a Canadian woman rather than return and be a burden. Then he puts on his single shoe, shoving the other under the bed, and hobbles off to start his new life as a recluse in the Northwest Territories.

These stories fill the weeks that go by without a shriek or a scene of interest. Weeks buried in soiled linens, blanket repair, soap theft and morning meetings where me and the other cleaners complain about our short break times, unflattering uniforms and the shitty coffee available in the staff room. But these times are mercifully punctuated by busy days where all hell breaks loose and the turbulence from across the city comes rolling into the lobby and rings the front desk bell announcing conventions, concerts, gatherings and parades; all good reasons for mayhem in my hotel.

Every fall I inevitably run into relations from up North when the annual Native festival rolls into town. It's an excuse for Indians from all over to pack up their regalia, call in sitters for the weekend and get to the Big City to kick up some shit and pick each other up. Being close to the stadium where the festival is held ensures that we are booked solid and that we won't have one of those eventless weeks.

Every year a hundred different people make their way into the rooms from reserves and Native communities all across the continent. And the stories that are played out here keep the staff talking long after and well into the Christmas season. I, of course, being the token Indian on staff, am called upon to mediate disputes, explain strange behaviour and to generally defend cousins and strangers alike.

It was at the tail-end of one of these festival weeks that I encountered my first body. It was in a corner room on the fourth floor. I think it was the smell that set my nerves on edge first. It smelt like the sea, or rather, like a sea full of rusty old barges. It was a solid, lonely smell that made me want to run. Once I turned on the lights and saw the body, leaking blood like oil from an old car, I wanted to run, but I couldn't. Instead I threw up into the pile of clean sheets I carried in my arms and stumbled, disoriented, down the hallway. I was still sitting on the radiator at the end

4

of the hall when a couple of guests walked by the open door and, probably attracted by that same sad, isolating smell, peeked in. Their screams brought the maintenance man, who then brought the Manager, who in turn brought the police. I slipped out the side door to smoke too many cigarettes while sirens and lights filled the world around me.

The girl jumped onto the bed, wearing underwear marked 'Wednesday' on a Sunday evening. She folded her spindly legs, bent like weary tulip stalks, over the edge, and peeled off the scab from her kneecap. And though she seemed to be unaware of the heavyset man standing by the door, she in fact watched him from behind her unevenly cut bangs. It was a game; this indifference, this comfort in uncomfortable moments; this actor's character she slid in and out of. She pulled the role on like a well-tailored suit, and, sauntering about, swung bony, bruised hips. She was cocky, in nothing but skivvies and a white wifebeater shirt made grey from a thousand washes in someone else's machine.

The man folded his bulk into a chair that faced the window looking out onto the non-descript building next door. She walked past him and rummaged around in her purse, producing cigarettes and a Zippo engraved with someone else's initials. She avoided contact with the man and instead sat crossed legged at the foot of the bed resting her head, still raw and jagged from last night's tequila.

As she lit up, she heard the stranger's voice from a million miles away, "This is a non-smoking room." She sneered at the man in the chair near the window that lead out to nothing. "I'm sure this is a non-whoring room too," she shot back. She took another drag, and then blew the dusty smoke intentionally in his direction. He looked back out the window as if distant and quaint shorelines lay there. She continued smoking and picked at the chipped blue nail polish on her nicotine stained fingers.

She hated him, this man, and these men: the ones who picked her up without expression and used her without emotion. The ones who picked her up with no more regard than they had for picking lint off the collars of their well-pressed suits. She preferred the sweaty nervousness of young virgins or the eager speediness of excited old vets with their knobby fingers and waxy breath to these cold, hard men. These were the ones who called her squaw. Who called her half-breed, the ones who would just as soon slap her than bother to put on the condom she always handed them. She often wondered why they didn't just keep the $80 it cost to be with her and drive their comfortable, bucket-seated SUVs home to the suburbs. They could kiss their wives hello and then slip into very hot showers to jerk off for free. Their peckish wives could use the money they saved spending an afternoon getting the silk wraps and pedicures that would goad them into putting out anyways. To these men she had no name and no face. She was a hole. Consequently, she held no regard for these bastards. She gave them the calculated respect accorded to dangerous dogs.

Her words hung between them, two strangers abandoned at the edge of the city in this unremarkable room; she could feel the tension in this storied space; she read it with her fingers like Braille. He had no patience. She, however, just wanted to sit for a minute, on this threadbare carpet in her 'days of the week' panties and enjoy a smoke before she was deposited back out onto the rainy corner where she would wait for the next car to slither up and empty out some engorged reptilian beast.

The man was hard and angular, the girl slick and indifferent, yet she couldn't help wanting to forge a connection in this insignificant room. She fought the urge to sit across from him in the matching chair with the round Formica table between them.

She thought back to her aunties holding council at the round, plastic-topped table back home. They gathered at that table as if smoking, laughing and sharing brown bottles of beer were a meal. They would suck on their Rothman's and their Players Filters and their 'roll-your-owns' through long afternoons. As a young girl she would often sit at the feet of her aunties under the table. Beside her would be the smelly old dog her Aunt Ida kept at her side like he was the reincarnation of her dead husband or a hairy old mole that wouldn't go away. She didn't think the dog even had a name. He was just there, silent and stinky with cheesy old fur and foggy grey eyes.

"I tell you, that ole witch up the hill there is up to her tricks again," Aunt Rose would say stubbing out the butt end of her smoke in the heavy cut crystal ashtray someone's nephew had given as a Christmas present. "I saw her out in the bush there behind her house the other day carrying an old packsack with her."

The 'ole witch up the hill' was a popular topic for these kitchen table councils. Sometimes the old lady up the hill was a crazy seer who used her powers against the people and kept the community in poverty. Other times she came from a long line of witches dating back to the early days of Europe where her grandmothers had sex with the devil in foreign fields and spent their nights eating little white children before hiding on the boat that came across the ocean to make the people sick.

The others 'harrumphed' and muttered, 'no good for sure' under their breath in agreement. And the young girl buried her nose in the dog's smelly fur and wondered what the ole witch could have had in her packsack that her aunties knew meant no good. Maybe she was burying body parts from the victims she silently plucked from beds at night like the metal claw that grabbed up toys in the game that came to town with the carnival every year. Or maybe her aunties were bored living in this place where nothing really happened and were just full of shit and the woman who lived on the hill was shy or sick of all the gossip. Maybe the packsack just meant that she was going on a picnic or something.

But who was the ole witch anyways? How long had she lived on that hill, the girl wondered. No one could say with any degree of certainty and though she asked, few ever gave a straight answer. One thing was for sure, without that ole witch, her aunties wouldn't have very much to talk about other than who snagged whom at the last party, who got arrested for bootlegging and when the next wedding was going to take place in the crooked old church with its lopsided crucifix that stabbed at the sky on Main Street.

But now she was here in this place and she doubted that the man who bought both her time and this room would want to sit at the table sharing smokes and stories about eccentric old women who lived back home. She pulled up her indifference towards this moment like a pair of socks and walked to the bathroom to chuck her smoke in the toilet.

Catching a piece of her reflection in the streaked mirror of the medicine cabinet, she decided to fix her smudged eyeliner as best as she could with two Q-Tips she found inside on the enamel shelves. She dabbed the ends into the slow trickle of water that poured from the tap.

She was young, high school young, but with the puffy eyes of a middle-aged woman who lived too hard and smoked too much. Her skin hid the sickness that crept through her blood despite the fact that leftover alcohol and freebased crack aggravated it. It looked soft and tanned even though she hadn't seen the sun in more than a few weeks; summer nights brought good business with the favourable weather and she lived in these dark hours. It was easier to sleep during the day when the straight folks scuttled between the office towers like smooth, black beetles scared away by the rougher skids that stole from these young workers foolish enough to nap in the park.

She quickly undid and re-braided her long brown hair, streaked with dye in lighter shades of red and coppery orange. Her dark eyes were smeared with turquoise eyeliner and sparkly powder shone across her sharp cheekbones. No lipstick. It got in the way of her duties. She was wide, but thin, too thin. She hadn't eaten a real meal since the street patrol came by the park with soup and some ham and butter sandwiches two days ago. A movement in the mirror caught her eye and she watched without breathing.

The man stood up, unfolded his limbs from their complacency, and stretched out until he filled the room with his long arms and cold blue eyes. She watched him from the mirror, breathing in shallow sips. She stayed quiet while she calculated like prey eyeing a passing hawk. Like the hawk, she measured the elasticity of time between hunger and her next meal. Guardedly, she secured her apathy and fastened it into place. She crossed the space between the bathroom and the bed smirking to show her superiority and demonstrate her control over this moment and every other moment that would come. This was, after all, her office, regardless of who leased out the space.

She hooked her thumb at the corner of her panties and tugged a bit, showing off the smooth line of hard muscle that ran down into her softest parts. As she did, the strap of her top slid off one shoulder and dipped playfully around the crook of her skinny arm. She was definitely a professional; the smoothness of both her switch to seduction and of the scar given by a former pimp that unfurled itself along her cheek attested to it.

Then the man did something odd, something that stole her smirk and drew a line on her forehead. He lay down on the bed, at once loosening his good silk tie and shifting his massive weight so that he could rest on his side, facing away from where she stood at the opposite half of the bed. She put her hands on angular hips and walked around the bed. There he laid, eyes closed, hand still loosening his tie, the other slipped into his pocket and secured his wallet. In a minute he was breathing deep and even. The line on her forehead expanded from the beginning of one eyebrow to the end of the other.

A greasy-faced clock fastened to the wall above the bed told her it was 11:46 p.m. She watched the beige plastic hands tick off time as the man fell deeper into his slumber on the uncomfortably anonymous bed. Perplexed, she slid down into a cross-legged squat on the threadbare carpet and held her head in her hands. She watched this man sleep. A troubled expression played around his smallish eyes. His receding blonde hair and badly pockmarked skin hinted of a virginal high school life.

Why would anyone pick up a hooker on a Sunday night in this huge city then take them to a chain hotel in a tourist part of town where the Yellow Pages escort girls got dibs out front, only to fall asleep? None of it made sense and for the life of her she couldn't formulate the pieces of this jigsaw puzzle to make out any sort of picture.

She lay down and pulled her slightly rug burned knees up to her chin, arms clasped together around her shins as though she were desperately trying to hold in her monstrously oversized gut. Her arms twisted anxiously, taking on a life of their own. She was eye level with the floor. She peered under the bed. She could see lint. Toward the headboard were some papers that had fallen behind it, some old betting forms and a page ripped from the phonebook. A nail file and an empty plastic cup with soft pink lips tattooed on the rim completed the picture. She closed her eyes.

One night she had a dream, which happened only very rarely these days and which was even rarer in the state she had injected, drank and smoked herself into. On this particular night she was passed out behind a strip joint with a head full of fumes and sticky fluids.

In her dream, she was sitting in a room, a wide room that smelt of cedar and heat. Her shoulders were bare and her hair was long and smooth, like the sleek ferns that grew down at the shore behind her auntie's house. Out the window she watched the full moon breathe as it sat in the sky—the wide, round, star-filled sky. A candle flickered from somewhere on a shelf beside her, throwing shadows on the wall. She watched them as they slid around each other, weaving in and out like masked dancers. And she saw there, dodging the other shadow men like a wild streak of wind, the shadow of her deceased brother. He moved with the erratic energy that had consumed him throughout his life. He threw his head back once in a while, long hair dipping low into the small of his back, and lifted watery grey arms to the sides of his face to laugh at the dancers around him, at the "crazy old Indians", unaware that he too was caught up in the dance.

From around her, she felt an immense quickening and then there were hands at her shoulders; two hands, belonging to two different women. She looked to her left and there stood a young woman with a serious face. She was wrapped in deep layers of material the same colour as the veins that snaked up and down her pale arms. She had sad smudges under her eyes as though a coal miner had tried to wipe away her tears in a moment of tenderness. Her dark hair was pulled back tightly into an intricate medicine wheel braid that took up every wave from her head and wove it into meaning. Her lips were thick and cut by deep creases symptomatic of a life spent outdoors in unforgiving sunlight and inside in dimly lit corners. She did not look unkind; she looked beautiful and fierce.

Then, the girl looked to her right. The hand that gripped her shoulder on this side belonged to an old woman; a woman whose severity and kindness ran down her face like the patterns of a butterfly's wings. In fact, almost everything about this woman reminded her of a butterfly. She looked so fragile in her age, yet ready to travel many miles before settling to rest. This woman held no weight at all in this room, yet she somehow filled every thing, every hollow space encased by the skin of something else. The girl felt the woman in her ears and mouth. The old woman was tangled in her hair and was crawling down her throat.

And then together, the two women reached down into the darkness and pulled out a cloak. They unfurled it with the air of a magician as though an important unveiling were occurring. They pulled it around the girl's shoulders. The cloak itself became a wide, round star-filled sky. Its weight was the weight of all eternity, from time immemorial passed down through slow migrations across eons and down the strands of DNA that brought everything to this moment. It was comforting, like the weight of a welcomed lover who has come home after many nights alone.

The girl woke up in the alley way, one stocking curled down around her worn heel, a strange boy stroking her heel's pale skin. She wept for all she had thrown away before really knowing it had existed. She cried so hard the strange boy left, tripping over broken-down boxes and over abandoned syringes. She cried until someone came and told her to fuck off and get the hell away from the building. She left, crying still, arms wrapped around her stomach. She cried for two days, until friends came by the blue building near the beer store where the hotel housing her room sat. They carried a case and a baggy with them. She promised herself, deep into the night and deeper into the baggy, that she would never dream again. Dreams were for pussies. Dreams didn't make you happy and they didn't make you money, so what was the point. She did remember, though, to walk down to the patch of glass-strewn beach at the bottom of her new city to put tobacco into the water on the anniversary of her brother's suicide, that crazy, cynical shadow dancer had killed himself. She went home and threw away the candles in her little room.

12:03 a.m.

What now then, (she wondered) at midnight, on a Sunday evening, lying fetal on the floor of a hotel room beside a sleeping stranger with a mere $3 to her name, the coins of which were folded in a tissue at the bottom of her bag? She stretched out an arm shrunk thin by neglect and toxic recreation and fiddled with the plastic cup under the bed. A small pool that smelt of sickly sweet whiskey dribbled out. Her mouth filled with saliva. Not that she necessarily enjoyed whiskey, but she did have an affinity for the amnesia it provided. And it would be something to do while her trick napped.

She pulled herself up from the carpet like one of those ladies who lunches at afternoon yoga classes, all bones and veins unraveling themselves from Downward Dog to a standing position. She pulled on her skirt and grabbed her bag. She was halfway through the door before she decided to take the room key. Maybe she'd check in on him later. A trick was a trick, after all, and if he was still here she could make some money and keep the room after they were done and he had shuffled home. Generally, the men didn't mind if she stayed in the rented rooms where they pushed and sweated over her, but some thought she had nothing better to do than attract attention to herself by incurring charges past check-out. These ones held the door open angrily as she pouted and slunk into her jeans like a kid late for school. She imagined herself this way, and if she went to school, she would be a pouty kid in too-big jeans, late every day.

She snatched the plastic key card off the bureau and crammed it into her bag. With an unusual touch of consideration that was as alien to her as waking up with the sun, she snapped off the light so the man could sleep without interruption. If he was still asleep when she got back, she could make her money and close off the night nicely.

She stood now in the hallway, a ridiculously nervous figure clutching a bag full of nothing, biting at stubby nails and tasting acrid flakes of blue nail polish. Her shoulders hunched in on themselves so much she was sure that if she really wanted to, she could pull them completely together. Perhaps she could flap them fast enough that they would carry her away, liberated by the bad posture of low self-esteem. She giggled at the image and caught herself laughing in the smudgy reflection of the brass plated elevator buttons. And for a moment, she didn't recognize the girl, the girl with the wings constructed of bones and fear, smiling an absurd sort of smile that was separate from the rest of her face.

Once she had laughed. Once she lived without the wall that had slowly built itself up inside the pit of her stomach, making it nearly impossible to laugh, to eat, swallow, shit, or even breathe. Her laughter bubbled up at odd moments. It came while sitting in the back of her uncle's truck crammed between cousins and dogs, when she was swinging from a branch half way up a tree in her great auntie's back yard and while someone drank too much or started a fight in the faded linoleum kitchen. Even when she came to the city and took her first handful of the multi-coloured pills that reminded her of the beads in her grandma's sewing box she laughed. But now that laughter was gone. She thought that maybe the ability to laugh and the ability to breathe were somehow dependent on each other because her breath was gone like a runner at the end of a lost race; a pointless and frustrating place to be.

She stopped laughing now. The girl in the smudgy brass reflection became solemn and filled with heaviness. She slid into the elevator and slipped down three stories, spilling out into the gaudily lit lobby with the fake flowers and polyester curtains. She slithered out the main doors and looped down the sidewalk with the steps of the very young or the very drunk. She was neither.

It took her twenty-five minutes to be sitting in front of a shot of tequila and a beer chaser, cigarette tucked behind her ear, admirer holding precariously to her elbow. She smiled at the buffet of inebriation that presented itself to her now and recalled pictures of her with feathered bangs. Pictures of her with friends and distant relatives in poster-covered rooms posing with half empty bottles lifted from parents' rooms, from behind the vegetable oil containers in the kitchen cabinet, from the back of uncles' closets. She remembered making 'monkey juice' in her grandma's base-ment from the dozens of bottles that lined the rec room, carefully pouring a thimbleful from each one and mixing them together in a rinsed out shampoo bottle to take to a sleepover down the street.

She remembered feeling like she was wearing a woolly toque on the inside of her skull, making everything fuzzy and kind of scratchy, yet warm and comforting, when she was felt up for the first time. It was in her best friend's basement, by her best friend's older brother while his friends watched. She remembered looking over his shoulder into the murky room with its splotchy old sofas, five boys in identical looking jeans lounging on them under clouds of cigarette and pot smoke. She remembered staring at the boy she had a crush on while he watched as his friend felt under her Tweety Bird shirt. She remembered lifting her shirt up so he could have a better look and feeling empowered and beautiful in his approving gaze. It was as though the boy who grew increasingly hard against her knee was just a tool. She didn't even pretend that he might have liked her. She certainly didn't like him, with his greasy chin and stubby fingers. She had said yes so she could avoid feeling bad about saying no.

The boys imagined her as easy, but she knew it was the game she play-ed with them was what was easy, not her. It was so easy to maneuver time and outcome with a peek of cotton panties from underneath her short striped skirt. It was so easy to get attention from unsupported cleavage while playing volleyball at recess rather than by having to share conversation and thought. She preferred it this way. Her breasts, her thighs, her mouth, these were all things that existed on the outside, in their world, far away from her own. She never did it for nothing. She always made sure of that —in her mind she came out on top. They got to finger her; she got a dime bag. They got a hand job; she got to have exciting plans for the weekend.

Other people made life hard. Girls waited for her after school to push her face into the asphalt and call her 'slut' and 'whore' while they stole her shoes and dumped sparkly nail polish in her hair. Boys waited until she was too drunk to walk before they loosened their jeans and took turns with her on her grandmother's sofa.

She stopped smiling and pounded back the tequila and half the beer before pausing for breath. She shook her admirer off after he had secured the next round (screwdriver and a Jagermeister) and rolled the cigarette across her lips like a thought.

She considered the man sleeping in the room. She pretended he was waiting for her, that he was a part of her life. It was nice thinking that someone was expecting her to come home. That he was wait-ing for her. She imagined him welcoming her return with a smile and a glass of juice. There would be clean blankets and a regular night of watching TV ahead. It was an uncomfortable thought that comforted her.

The bar was, of course, dimly lit with a fine layer of indiscriminate grime covering everything the way tendrils of smoke used to before the smoking ban came into effect. A woman beside her picked up lemon slices from the bartender's container near the register and threw them back down. (She made a mental note not to order any more mixed drinks where lemons would be included.) The man, who had ordered her drinks, slunk back to his table where two of his sad looking friends awaited his return. They greeted him with hails of Caesar for even getting as far as to be allowed to buy drinks for such a young, pretty thing. Then they returned to their monotone chatter of cubicles and weekend football games like giant, slightly paunchy rats over a hunk of prime cheese. Then she saw her.

At first she didn't really notice this table, or the woman who sat tall and imposing in the farthest recesses of the corner of the bar. She slowly became corporeal, like an image becoming clear to eyes that are just getting used to the dark. She was a wide woman with serious shoulders and something familiar about the way she folded her hands together like a student at a wooden desk. The girl half expected to see the flash of a uniform kilt under the table and a pencil tucked behind an ear. But instead, she saw the folds of a voluminous skirt in an intricate geometrical pattern, the same pattern she had noticed back home decorating girls' hand drum bags and old men's jackets.

There was something so familiar about this woman in a city where she knew no other Native person besides some of the skids who hung out in the park. These were the unrelated cousins who bummed cigarettes off her and offered swigs from obscured bottles nestled deep in the folds of anonymous brown paper bags. There were a few Native organizations in the neighbourhood where she could get a lunch, or a shower or even some new clothes. Some would help with training or employment if she walked into the fluorescent lit reception areas with framed Native art hung crookedly on beige walls. But she didn't want to go there. What the hell did she need a job for, she had one. And she couldn't go back to school. She just couldn't. And what if they tried to make her talk to an Elder? How could she form the words and tales of her days and nights to such a respectable person who could never understand what she did or how she lived? What was there on the other side anyways?

She would sit sometimes, and watch the women in their long skirts go in and out of the main doors of the women's place across from the park. They would share cigarettes or sit on the front steps with paper plates balanced on their knees, feeding children bits of fry bread and laughing. Sometimes she heard them singing at the full moon or coming out to offer their tobacco at the base of the large tree that stood out front, providing shade in the hot summer afternoons. She sat in the park, on the other side of the road, sweat beading her upper lip, waiting for nightfall to bleed inky colour into the pale, pale sky. She offered her tobacco to her greedy lungs and shut out the drumbeats with the pounding of her own heart while the pills shut her eyes from the inside out.

Who was this woman, this tall familiar woman? She was too curious to let it go, but too paralyzed by doubt to approach. The indecision and curiosity angered her and she swung back the shot and exhaled too loudly. The lemon picker looked up and paused before dropping another slice back into the bowl.

When it finally hit her who the woman was, all there was left in the world as it tunnelled down on her was the dilation of pupils and a sharp intake of breath. The girl stared straight forward and it took a full minute before the low ebb of the bar's music returned and the sounds of the strangers around her closed back in. Their jagged conversations tumbled across her lap like clumsy puppies. She knew this woman and had felt those hands, the ones that even now lay folded on a chipped wooden table like the gesture of a demure schoolgirl. She was the woman on the left... the woman from her dream, the dream that made the boy run away from her in that alleyway. And she was watching her now from the corner of this dimly lit bar. She could feel her cold eyes circled with dark smudges as if she had never slept nor had ever needed to. "Do dead people need sleep?" the girl suddenly wondered.

She wanted to bolt from this place full of near dead Indians sitting at corner tables. She felt fear slip its scaly tentacles into her ears and around her thighs. It was a desperate, intrusive feeling. She tried to will her legs to move but they remained frozen to the spot, pinning her to the barstool as if they were old rubbies bent on drinking away the night there. She knew the woman was still there and was staring straight into her; she could feel it. At least her arm was still working. It picked up her drink and served it to her quivering lips who behaved well enough to procure the alcohol for the awaiting ball of terror that had been thrown over the fence of her stomach and lie there now with no intentions of leaving.

Tinny soft rock from a busted speaker lingered over the guffaws and snorts from a table of drunken office workers, their hair permed and fake nails painted in horrid tones of red and orange polish. Chair legs rubbed against tiled floor and excuses to go to the bathroom peppered the quiet barroom. There was football and cubicle talk and a monstrous apparition calmly sitting in the corner with folded hands and shadowed eyes.

That was it. The girl couldn't do it anymore. Her heart would explode like she had just been struck by the touch of death in some '70s kung fu movie. She felt panic, which was much rawer than fear; panic made it impossible to react to her fear. Her legs were being woken up from some deep slumber by invisible needles and she suddenly felt that she had to move. In fact, she was just now starting to stand. "Good," she breathed, relieved that she could now make an escape, "good." She nervously pulled back some strands of hair that had come loose and clung to her sweaty face.

Things were working out now. She had her purse over her shoulder, a shoulder still knotted and twisted with apprehension. She was turning, eyes carefully focused on the door. It was in sight and she was swimming out of paralysis towards it.

"Shit!" she cursed out loud, mouth opening and closing like a fish out of water. She wasn't walking to the door. She was fighting against currents, being buffeted and dragged by an invisible undertow, stiffly making her way to the corner table as if she were a child's pull toy. *Terror.* She could only dig fingernails into the plastic leather of her bag and clench her teeth together so they didn't chatter like the soft pecking of fake fingernails on an office computer. The woman at the table stared straight ahead, almost through her. In fact, the girl thought that perhaps the woman was unaware of her and everything around her, but then she smiled, a wide, full smile that flashed rows of little sharp teeth and dug fleshy grooves into the soft charcoal around her eyes. "Ahneen."

Her voice was a key that unlocked a red torrent of memory and the girl fell down. She watched in horror as the bar's dirty floor beneath her disappeared. Something inside of her broke open at ripped seams and she slipped in the pool it made at her feet like viscous blood poured out in a violent accident. She clutched at the table, fingers trying in vain to keep her head above the surface. The woman reached across the table and loosened her fingers, smiling with her tiny teeth, eyes darker now, sparkling like stars in the sky. And then the girl was gone.

Now she was under the table, but the table wasn't the same. There was no gum wadded under here left to dry like fossilized glue. The music was gone and the lemon picker had disappear-ed. There were no office workers or bloated men. Instead, there was a familiar smell and an ancient runny-eyed dog who licked her face solemnly, almost mechanically as if he had always been there. She heard the clunking of brown bottles above her and saw pudgy feet wrapped in knitted slippers all around her. She heard her aunties laugh like good-natured sorcerers and knew where she was.

And so she did what she always did, she stayed very still and very quiet, listening to the tales that these women wove into the wooden ceiling above her like meticulous carvers with very small instruments.

"Harrumph, what are you going to do about the girl," Ida asked, sliding a bottle back and forth between her cracked, brown hands. Gladys shuffled her feet like cards and sighed, "I'm gonna do what I've always done. I'm going to keep watchin' her until her good for nothing mother returns for a week or two and then dumps her back into my lap."

Aunt Rose slammed a fist down hard and the table shook. The dog whimpered a bit and laid a greying muzzle on dirty paws. "It's not right. Rita might as well just stay in the goddamn city for all the good she does when she comes back here."

"Where's the girl's father anyways? I heard she doesn't even know who he is." A soft chuckle escaped that wasn't really a laugh but rather a snorting reproach.

Gladys took a long sip. "I do."

The others were silent for a full minute before Rose communicated their mutual shock and annoyance. "As if you do! Who then?"

There was more sniffing and sipping as if Gladys was preparing for a great speech and the others gave her the respect of such. She drew herself up, bottom half waddling under the table to sit very straight. The girl was straining so hard, that she felt her ear pop and minute sounds like the rushing of air out of the dog's nose came screaming in. She had never heard much about her mother. Her father was a ghost to her, not real at all.

By the time her auntie finally spoke the girl was leaning so far towards the voice that she almost fell into a wide, aproned lap. "'Member when that ole witch went away for those few years, when her place was boarded up and we had to keep chasing away those kids from goin' up there to fool around?"

The others nodded so hard, the girl was sure she could hear their necks creaking.

"She went to the city for a while. Met a man and followed him there. He was a white man who worked for the government no less." She paused to drink and the others grew irritated in the pause. "Anyways, she got pregnant and he left her… of course. Shognosh always do."

The other women sucked their teeth and mumbled about the transient nature of good for nothing white men.

"Anyways, she had a son. I heard it from old Gertie, before she passed on last year. At first I thought it was crazy talk, you know. I mean, how can you believe a woman who insulates her house with boxes of empties?"

The others laughed and there were faint clicking noises as cigarettes were lit and smoke made its way under the table as hands reached down to pull up slippers and scratch at the dollar store pantyhose they wore. The second aunty replied, a hint of affection in her voice, "Yeah, what an Indian savings account that woman had!" There was more laughter. Finally one had a coughing fit and Gladys resumed her story.

"Anyways. The boy grew up in the city with his daddy's mother. And the ole witch came back home, having no ties to her own flesh and blood." They all clucked their tongues and mumbled about how only witches and good for nothing's could abandon their own children, and the girl wondered if this meant that her mother was a witch.

"Anyways, Rita hooked up with him when she went there to look for work. And you know the rest. She comes home bigger than a house, ready to burst. Has the girl and then leaves for the city as if she just came home to drop off some luggage. She's my burden now," she replied with nobility in her voice, a martyr for being such a selfless guardian.

The others mumbled their acknowledgement of her sacrifices before one threw up her heavy arms and wailed, "Tabernacle! That means that ole witch is the girl's grandmother!!" The others threw hands over mouths and there were sharp intakes of breath. The storyteller shushed them violently, "Be quiet you, you'll wake the girl!" They all looked over at the couch where the small shape of a sleeping child under a yellow crocheted blanket turned over, deeper into the soft cushions of the brown velour couch in the attached living room.

The girl under the table was confused. Who was that? She got up from under the table carefully and stretched to her full height, not caring whether or not her aunties would give her shit for hiding under the table again, but they didn't seem to even notice her. They kept on talking, this time in Ojibway and in softer tones, hunkered down now, the ashtray between them all like a sharp edged crystal ball. She tiptoed over to the child and peered down at her, her dark hair tangled in moist fingers, body curled around a flat, round cushion that stunk of stale smoke and cheesy dog. She pulled a bit at the corner of the blanket and looked into her own face.

"What the fuck…" she managed to shriek, looking down at herself as a small child, sleeping fitfully on her auntie's old couch, before the room collapsed in on itself and her eyes couldn't hold a single image steady. It was as if the small apartment, the last in a row of four at the end of a gravel road, was being ripped from its foundations, Wizard of Oz style. The girl threw herself over the smaller her, still sleeping, unaware of the chaos, and closed her eyes.

When she opened them again, everything was dark and from somewhere the sound of music belched out of a broken speaker. She stood up very quickly and smacked her head on the underside of a table crusted with fossilized gum. And then someone was shouting, "Hey, hey you, time to go now." From the bar, the lemon picker giggled and the bartender, flourishing under the picker's attention, continued, "You can't handle your booze; you gotta get the hell outta here. No napping under the tables, eh."

The girl crawled on bruised knees and looked around. Her aunties were gone. The dog had disappeared and she was alone at the bar where office workers drank sugary cocktails and complained loudly of the bosses they would never confront. She felt as if she had just returned from a long journey and the jet lag made her movements unfamiliar and difficult. The armchair quarterbacks still sat at their table like greasy rodents, but her admirer was now averting his eyes, not wanting to be associated with the seemingly drunk girl on the floor. She stood and brushed pretzel crumbs and straw wrappers off her skirt. Everything was the same, except of course that the starry eyed woman that had thrown her into the quicksand on the floor and brought her to her auntie's house was now gone.

She pulled her purse up over her shoulder once more, flipped the bartender the finger and left.

Outside the air was cold. She pulled her jacket closed and threw a shoulder into the biting wind. She felt a shortness of breath, as though she had just run a long distance across uneven ground. She felt unwell. There was pain from somewhere deep inside of her, a pain she had felt before but something she couldn't quite recall. She didn't know where she was going. She was done drinking for the night, that was for sure. There was no way she was going to risk going into another bar with a chance of running into that crazy old ghost. The thought of those black eyes like shining empty sockets made her shudder.

She walked south, realizing that she was heading in the direction of the hotel. She reached into her pocket and wrapped cold, clammy fingers reassuringly around the key card that was nestled there among condom wrappers and a broken cigarette. Yeah, that's where she would go, back to her room, back to her job.

Fuck these revelations about a past she cared nothing for. She had work to do. Who gave a shit about who her father was anyway? She did remember her mother and her brief visits well enough to know that family reminiscing was only more fodder for a fire that made her try desperately to put it out with bottles of flammable liquids. Jack Daniels made a lousy firefighter. And she didn't want to drink anymore. At least not tonight with the fucking Indian Morticia Addams inviting herself out as a drinking buddy, giving her visions and shit.

She turned down a tree-lined side street, nodded hello to a work-er huddled on the corner in a shiny red dress whose knees were rub-bing against each other like sticks seeking fire and found a dark step to sit on. She pulled out the broken smoke and a small baggy and tried to roll a joint with fingers that didn't want to follow or-ders. She rested them on her stomach for a moment, her hard, cold stomach. It felt like a kettle full of icy well water. She managed to glue together two wrinkled papers from the bottom of her bag and had sprinkled the crumbs of weed she had left in them when she felt eyes on her. She slowly looked up, both hands holding her project, and was getting ready to yell at whatever moocher or good Samaritan had decided to bug her now.

And then the green dust and shredded tobacco were on the step where her feet rested, like rice thrown at a wedding. The papers were blowing away in the bitter wind, graceful as a dove released into the clear blue sky. She forgot to breathe and her face tightened her mouth in a little round 'o'. At the foot of the stairs, with a look of recognition and expectancy was an old woman whose severity and kindness ran identically down her face.

The air around this grandmother buzzed angrily like flaps of thick plastic taped to a broken car window, snapping and fighting the rushing wind. And she knew that somehow this woman did not belong in this air, that she was a slow image peeping through rips, while the world around moved at incredible speed.

This was the woman on the right from her prophetic dream, the same dream from which one ghost had already escaped. The girl felt an odd sensation in her kettle-like stomach. It was as if holes were punched in the walls of her blood vessels. She felt the blood seeping into the spaces of her body and she knew that she must be dying. Her head pounded her mouth was as dry as old newspaper. The spirit at the bottom of the stairs turned and walked calmly across the street; the air charged with electricity all around her. And the girl was following her. Once again her legs were operating on a remote, seemingly controlled by the smooth steps of the old lady. She heard her heart in her ears and out of the corner of an eye she saw shadows dancing to the pounding she heard in her head.

"Trevor," she whispered her brother's name. It slipped out from between frozen lips like a leaf skidding across an empty parking lot on a blustery morning, no direction or meaning. But none of the shadows responded. They remained only energy pushed into existence by an old lady, who now, with arthritic unease, lowered herself onto a park bench across the street. The girl found herself collapsing into a cross-legged, child-like position on the sandy ground at the woman's feet. Her eyes swung about frantically in her fixated head, unable to focus, unable to find escape. And the old woman smiled a soft, toothless grin that should have brought comfort. But as she reached out with mittened hands, the girl felt her breath caught somewhere beneath her small breasts. Then one soft, deer hide covered hand covered each of her ears and the world was erased like a pencil drawing.

Now there was a house, a leaning house with weathered, chipped white paint and a half-finished front porch. The rusted gutter hung like an obscene broken finger from the side. The front window was curtained with a faded Star Wars bed sheet. But the trees that embraced this old mushroom of a house were imposing and strong and leant the abode an air of importance and mystery. It was as if it were an artifact from another time and place, transported here, telling in its imperfections. To repair the gutter or to add a railing to the frame of the porch would change its nature and it would become just another home on a dirt road instead of the storybook it was.

The girl saw her own hand reaching out to knock on the door and tried in vain to recoil. The sound was hollow and far away, as if she had cotton balls jammed into her ears, or the image of the house was wrapped in cloth. She felt as though she were knocking on a tapestry of a house hanging on a clothesline in someone's backyard.

The screen door shook as the heavy wooden inside door was pulled open. At once she knew where she was though she had never been allowed to go there during the daylight hours of her youth. There, smaller than she could have ever imagined she really was, was the ole witch from up the hill. Something in her broke and spilled out into her head. She felt red tinged tears slide down her pale cheeks. "Nokomis?" she questioned the small, apple doll-looking woman and this ole witch from up the hill who stood on the other side of the screen.

There was no reply, only the sound of the screen door opening and a rush of warm air rubbing the girl's frozen face. She stepped in. The witch was now retreating down the dim hallway, a soft curve under a man's oversized cable knit sweater that may have been white at some point in time.

In the kitchen she sat at a round wooden table, much like the one her aunties converged upon, like the three witches of Macbeth, to stir the mythology of this dusty little place. She carefully sliced through a brick of canned headcheese with a plastic knife and placed two portions onto chipped tea saucers. The girl was unsteady now and sat down opposite the old lady, who unlike her aunties in the last visit, seemed to be fully aware of her presence. She was very still while the woman poured two mugs of weak tea. The girl wrapped her icy fingers around the warm mug, adorned with a faded Petrol Canada logo. The old woman's mug had a cartoon of a smiling green vegetable that was preaching, *"Beans. They make the going great!"*

The girl examined the kitchen, looking for signs of the mysterious doings that kept this woman a top protagonist in this village of stories. The floor was a patchwork of four or five different types of linoleum; each equally scratched and faded from sun, and scraping chair legs, hard soled shoes and the sharp nails of outdoor dogs. The walls were bare except for a plaque with the words, *"God bless this mess,"* burned into the wood with clumsy precision. There was a musty smell in the air that wasn't unpleasant.

Then there came a noise from down the hall of someone dragging hobbled legs and approaching on pins and needles. And into the light came a tall woman with long, thin hair that wrapped around the buttons of her flannel shirt and snaked through the hoops in her ears. She wore too-big slippers to match the old lady's too-big sweater and was decidedly hung over. It was Rita, the girl's mother.

The girl stood there, surprise and shock shoved adrenaline into her veins. She sipped in air like very strong whiskey and cringed at each breath. It was her mother! What the fuck was her mother doing here? What the fuck was she doing here? And then her mother, in an act more intimate than any she had performed outside of giving birth–and even that was drug induced–walked directly through the girl. She felt momentary warmth and the sounds of irregular heartbeats, cats screaming, tires squealing, bones snapping, punches landing on flesh and strange bugs chirping all twisted up together into one thick audio rope. And that was when she realized that she was not really here, that the old woman did not see her there. That the gross, slightly gelatinous slice of headcheese was not for her and that the Petro Canada mug was meant for someone else. Her mother.

"Whaddya open the door for?" the woman groaned, holding the table for balance as she sat down in the chair that was only seconds before occupied by her daughter, or some smoky doppelganger of her, some dream daughter as real and unreal as a fetus buried deep inside a fallopian tube.

The old woman took a bite of her snack and looked out the window into the grey spaces beyond and muttered, "Only letting in some fresh air, that's all." And she pulled her eyes around the room, catching the girl's eyes so briefly she thought perhaps that she had been spotted ... but she couldn't be sure. And they ate and drank in silence for a few minutes before the old lady spoke again, "Heard from your girl lately?"

Her mother jumped a bit, as if she had just seen the ghost that stood behind her chair at that very moment. She actually stammered and fiddled around with her cup, swiping it across the smooth surface of the table that seemed to stretch for miles between the two women like a bored kitty with a new toy. "I, ah, wha...why would you ask me that?" She didn't wait for an answer. "We haven't spoken in a while. I think she's still in the city."

"Harrumph," the old lady jerked her head as if belching out her disapproval with great effort and sounding a lot like the women down the hill who threw their heads back and belched out disapproval back up the hill. "She needs you."

There was a loud crack as the mug careened past the bored kitty's outstretched paw and went smashing to the floor. Tea trickled through the cracks in the linoleum like large rivers seen from space. "Don't give me any more of your voodoo bullshit, Elsie. I'm sick of it. I only came here to dry out a bit, to get my shit together before I head out West to meet up with my ole man", and then, "Jesus." She swore as punctuation.

The old woman didn't even seem to notice the tea's river map stretching out across her floor. "Your girl is more important than hanging out in Winnipeg, drinking with some no good Cree and his cousins." She rose, very slowly like a building being constructed on a downtown corner. "Your girl is meant for great things, much more than you or I. She needs guidance, that's all."

The mother sneered, "Yeah, yeah, greatness. The same way I was before your good for nothing brat Dad knocked me up, eh." She laughed through her teeth like a bull snorting at a particularly scrawny matador.

The girl was unmoving, not only because she could effect no change on this scenario, but because the strange condition that had gripped her from earlier on in the evening was slowly but surely gaining foot. She felt certain now that she was dying. Her pulse was quick and fluttering, her tummy was extended and sore, her head screamed at her and she felt as if she would pass out from nausea and the constant internal yelling. She could feel the blood draining out of her veins and into her spongy flesh. She could feel her death sliding in like an automatic door had shuttled open somewhere in her will allowing its easy entrance. But she was a mere shadow in this woman's kitchen, in her grandmother's house, and shadows can't die.

The old woman threw a faded tea towel onto the spilt tea and approached her guest without the Martha Stewart recommended gentile nature, putting a sagging arm on either side of the woman who tried to back away now though she didn't move an inch. "Girl. That was your greatness." Then, amazingly, the woman stared past her mother, almost through her very skull and into the eyes of the shaking, time-displaced visitor, "She needs to come home."

And then it was over. The old woman was scooping up cold tea off an old floor. The girl's mother was fetching more in a different mug, this one painted faded pinkish red with another corporate logo spelt across it. She loaded up her, '*I want to be a Toys " Я " Us kid*' mug, and lit a cigarette off the stove, softly shaking her head, almost unperceivably, a mute protest to the old woman's prophecy.

Then the girl was being pulled away like a giant had inhaled her from behind. She felt her shirt go first, then her hair slipped through an airy cervix, relief and tension at once in the transfer. Her feet went last, which is why her landing back into reality was not an easy one, being whipped through rips and epochs by the seat of her pants.

She felt like a comb being run through very tangled hair as she pulled herself out of this vision and back into real time. When she finally cleared away the clouds from her eyelids and felt the sandy ground beneath her bared thighs, it was like reaching the bottom of the knot, and she was thrown out the end with considerable force. The bruises would come later when she was already nestled in the comfort of a chiropractically correct bucket seat, sliding across ribbons of highway in a climate controlled Greyhound.

And of course, the butterfly woman was gone, though wisps of sweet smoke stretched out their tendrils like a faded projection from a far off movie house. The girl pulled herself up quickly, though there was no need. There were no lemon pickers or sarcastic bartenders here in this empty lot, just dried, crunchy leaves underfoot, scraps of paper and a girl whose skirt had been hiked up as though she had just come down a very steep slide to land in this sandy spot.

Disoriented, a bit grubby and a lot confused, she felt better nevertheless. Her fingers were no longer numb and the close to bursting girth of her tight belly had subsided. She still wore the painful red tourniquet of a headache, but it no longer threatened to send her reeling to the train tracks to lay her neck across cold, steel rail in hopes of completely severing herself from the problem. No, there was nothing supernatural about this headache. She might even be able to control it with some speed and a couple Tylenols. And so it was with a bit of relief and the underlying cheerfulness of someone who had just escaped certain death that she scrambled to her feet and started across the street towards the hotel and its sleeping custodian.

Each time she stepped closer to the building where he lay, the girl managed to make him bigger in her mind. He was no longer an average, middle-aged white man of medium build. He was a huge, corpulent Lord, in whose terrible and tight fisted reign her small spirit would soon be crushed. He was the embodiment of every man who had ever pushed his way into her; into her space; into the place from which she had removed her scared items. It was a cave of ice. It was nothing more than a crevice in the side of an unmoving mountain. She was sick of housing dusty travellers and unconscious animals acting out of instinct and sweaty, procreative need.

And now this sleeping giant, this traveller from some suburb where everything was shades of beige and of medium height, weight, size, strength, quality, build, temperature, income, expense, interest and lifespan was sure to want to crawl inside her cave. This unconscious rat was sure to want to hibernate away from whatever ill winds blew him to this part of town. And though she felt like a prisoner released, she knew she had to return. It seemed as though he was the last link she could see to any sort of reality or sanity. She had to reassure herself of the existence of this world and her place in it, to reassure herself that there was no merit to the visions of this night.

Aside from feeling liberated and in remission from her strange death, the girl felt disoriented and confused. What did it all mean? What was the woman talking about, 'coming home'? What did that even mean for her anymore? She had a job here. She had friends here. She belonged in the room she rented with the particleboard bureau and the cracked mirror. She belonged in hotel rooms with strange men. Maybe. She couldn't make a definite decision on direction. It inflamed her already sore head. So she just kept moving towards the hotel and the sleeping man, the man who would pay her for a couple minutes of meaningless physicality. Thinking about seeing her family was more painful than anything she could do in this city, to or by herself.

The girl looked up, hands stuffed into her pockets, chin tilted towards the glowing neon moniker of the hotel. She breathed foggy air back out into the crisp night from exhausted lungs and whispered, "Honey, I'm home." She looked up into the fourth story windows trying not to see the big, great sky beyond, trying not to see all the possibilities of this wide, open sky. Only the room and her job. Walking into the hotel, everyone seemed haunted, haggard and two-dimensional. She felt like she hadn't come home at all.

She pulled out the card key as she passed the front desk so as to assuage any doubt that she belonged here in this uniform place, in this anonymous dorm. An elevator hummed as it pulled her body back up four stories and deposited her like a baby in a basket on the doorstep. She whimpered just a bit before she shrugged up the corners of her 'anonymous girl' cape, tossing her head back into the capacious hood that rendered her faceless, nameless – a great fucking businesswoman.

She paused for just a moment before swiping the key through the slot of door 414. She saw her aunties' legs and her small sleeping body on a brown velour couch. She saw the harsh face of dark-eyed apparition and the sweet concern on the face of the butterfly woman, sitting on an inner city park bench with a tired little hooker at her knee as if it were story time in a kindergarten class revolving around a different sun in an alternate universe. She saw her Nokomis wishing her return. Then she saw her life here, devoid of thought.

People all over the world at this very moment were dying for their right to more than exist, their right to live as free people, to think and feel and cry and dance. They bled for these small and beautiful freedoms. To peel potatoes in their own kitchens and hold on tightly to sweet, sweaty lovers in twisted sheets under skies they could never see from the inside of cement jail cells. She fought to exist and not to live. She was dying for it. She was slowly bleeding over years of pills, needles, punches, and bruised thighs. Bail bought in backseats of cruisers. Park benches, sticky joints and dried out cigarettes. She was dying for the freedom not to live. And once again she was opening the door into her own cell. And it didn't seem so horrible. After all, as long as she could see all the walls close in around her, she knew no one else could walk through them.

The first thing she noticed was the smell. The room smelt of iron and steel. It smelt of wet nails and rusty buckets. The odor was overpowering in its tightly compressed nature. She saw old metal rowboats, quietly decomposing, tied to crooked, creaking docks when she inhaled. She heard silverware tumbling over each other in a crowded kitchen drawer when she exhaled. Everywhere was the smell of toolboxes and fishing lures. It was even in the carpeted suite on the fourth floor of her temporary home. Above the smell hovered the absolute absence of noise.

She switched on the overhead light. The man lay very still on the bed. His eyes were still closed, his hand still shoved into his pocket to cover the contents of his billfold wallet. Streaking down from his nostrils, pooling thick and gooey around the indents of his upper lip, were stains and dried matter left from steady streams of thick red blood flecked with the odd piece of mucous or some other viscous liquid. There were drying puddles in the folds of his neck. Each eye was turned into a bottomless reflecting pond. Unfortunately, oceans of blood had poured from his rectum, from behind his nails, from his ears and the spaces in between his puffy gums and yellowed teeth. Even then, blood made his knees and joints swell like water balloons. His toes were engorged. His stomach was hard and protruding. He was still, like a monumental water fountain suddenly shut down for the evening.

The girl turned ever so slightly and threw up in the beige plastic trash receptacle under the counter nearest to the door–quietly, so as to not disturb the body on the bed. It wasn't the sight of all the blood that hitched up her stomach; rather, it was the thought of the internal violence that must have occurred in this room over the past few hours while she walked the streets feeling as if she were dying, feeling that every seam inside her body and the casings to each organ had ripped open like torn sausages and were spilling blood into corners and crevices. She felt this death. This death had slipped away like a loose silk scarf on a windy day, blowing about the city to carelessly land on the shoulders of someone else, here in this room.

She was released. Hands that had been cupped around her as if she were a tiny bird had opened to the sky. She stretched upwards, shaking out stiff, cold hands and made her way to the bed. She held her breath and, giggling a bit at her own nervousness, reached into the man's pocket, loosening lukewarm fingers made sticky with coagulated platelets. She pulled out his wallet and removed four twenties, their edges crusted with blood smudged around a dead American president she could not name.

On her way to the bus station, she wiped off the blood that left fingerprints on everything she touched, around her mouth as she smeared off caked lipstick, on her purse as she tossed in the money, on her jacket when she clutched it closed to the wind that had suddenly picked up and pushed at her back. She rubbed at the strange half moon patterns flowered across her chest. She constantly checked her own pulse, making sure she wasn't an animated corpse running down rain-slicked streets towards an impossible future back home. Now the cape she shrugged up over her shoulders and tossed over her head was the wide, round star-filled sky itself, and she was running towards it as fast as she could.

room 502

When people die in certain places, those places are irrevocably changed. It's as if the stories of their death become imprinted on the walls or are thrown up on the ceiling like a film projection. The dead's tales fall across the bed like long hair and tangled limbs. Sometimes when people die, the rooms they die in become tombs even after the body is removed.

I'm reminded of tombs when I'm in Room 502 now. The bathroom never seems bleached clean, the kind of clean that makes a person feel comfortable enough to actually sit on the toilet seat or put a toothbrush on the sink counter. Whenever I make the bed, the corners wrinkle and the comforter feels oily, like it's only made it halfway through the rinse cycle. And those annoying lamps that stick out from the walls like engorged sconces give out a weaker kind of light. It's as if electricity has no place in this room and only the dodgy illumination of torches would do.

I was not the first one to find the body this time. I was in the laundry room smoking a roach with Carlos, the kid who sweeps out the basement at night and steals soap and detergent for his elderly mom before he leaves in the morning. Carlos is a good kid with great weed, making him a natural choice for me to spend break times with. In fact, I didn't hear the guy in 502 had died until Marie came swooping into the room like a flustered hen, arms up in the air, the fat flaps that hang under them swinging wildly like useless wings. "Oh My God! Oh My God! Oh My God!" she screeched as I fanned the sticky smoke out of the air. Carlos quickly doused the joint and put it in the breast pocket of his uniform shirt.

"What? Jesus Marie, calm down," I grabbed her shoulders to steady her, but her eyes kept roaming around in her head like a little bobble-headed doll. "What is it?"

"Another body. They found a body up on the fifth floor." And then she was off again, fretting down the hallway to the coffee room to share the story with her cousins who worked the big laundry machines and washed the thousands of towels and sheets to be stacked onto the industrial racks each day. Her arm wings swung silently as she made her way down the hall, making her look as if she were performing an absurd sort of jitterbug.

Carlos and I exchanged a meaningful glance. He crossed himself as I picked up my stack of clean linens from the laundry table and hurried off to the fifth floor. I walked to the elevator, listening closely to the frantic whispers from behind the front desk as I passed through the lobby. The clerks were gossiping with the guy who filled the vending machines.

"Suicide."
"Overdose."
"How are we going to explain the police to the guests?"
"Never seen him before."
"She went to deliver the extra towels he called down for, poor woman."

I rode in silence and slipped out of the elevator and into the hallway before the police arrived. The Manager and a few of the cleaning staff were stressing by the door to Room 502. It was clear by the way they spoke that they were feeling important like VIPs at a very somber event. It was as if they were CSI specialists.

"Clearly there was no foul play here. No forced entry, no distur- bances. And see how the needle is down by his right side? Obvi- ously it fell out of his own hand after injection," Detective Sergeant Night Manager postulated.

"Yes, clearly. Also there doesn't seem to be any motive otherwise. No extra drugs about, no money missing as far as I can tell. Yes, I agree. It was most definitely a suicide," concurred Special Agent Maintenance Supervisor.

"Funny how they never manage to untie the tourniquet before they go," Coroner Cleaning Lady said as if this were the thou- sandth suicide she had presided over instead of just harbouring a secret passion for police dramas. "It's that fast and effective."

Truth was, I had more than a voyeur's interest in this room and its deceased guest. I had met the man a few weeks back on one of my rounds. There was no 'Do Not Disturb' sign hanging on the knob, and after knocking twice, I had let myself in.

The room was damp and smelled like decaying flowers. The blinds were drawn, so I picked my way across the cluttered floor to open those first. Turning the crank to let in some natural light, I thought I heard water draining from the bath. Without get- ting the blinds all the way open, I turned around, and there was a naked man standing in the bathroom door, a blue towel tied around his skinny waist. I was a little startled but far from scared. The man looked like he was having difficulty even just standing there, so I felt no fear of an impending attack.

"Well," he moved carefully over to the unmade bed, "I'm not re- ally sure what to say in this situation." He sighed deeply as he lowered his upper body onto the pile of pillows that were stacked up against the headboard.

"I can come back later," I shuffled over towards the door.

"No, no," he said with eyes half shut. "I don't mind. And besides this room could use some attention, I suppose."

I don't usually work in front of guests. It's a little unprofessional and can get more than a bit creepy. Plus, I hate making small talk. But I was already behind in my rounds and this guy looked like he was going to pass out any minute, so I figured, why not?

I tackled the bathroom first, picking up used towels and chucking them into the bin attached to my cleaning cart, that I had wheeled in from the hallway. I threw out the empty shampoo bottles and the half cake of cracked soap from the bottom of the tub. I scrubbed the toothpaste off the counter, sprayed and wiped the mirror and placed fresh towels and toiletries around the room.

When that was done, I made my way back out to the bedroom. The man was fast asleep on the bed. His legs were so thin I could see the tendons sticking out around his ankles and his kneecap looked painfully large under the parchment skin. He was curled up in a half fetal position with the blue towel still knotted around his waist. His hair looked downy, like a duckling's back, and there were deep burrows under his closed eyes. He was clearly sick and I wondered what was wrong. I had just turned my back on him when I got my answer.

"Cancer," he said, eyes still closed.

I jumped a bit, "Pardon me?"

"Cancer," he opened his brown eyes. "You were staring at me in that way that people do when they are asking themselves questions. I'm dying of cancer." He folded his arms behind his head now like a mischievous boy and managed a half smile.

"I'm sorry, I didn't mean to stare." I was uncomfortable now and just wanted to finish up this room so I could leave.

"It's okay," he mumbled. "Could you do me a favour and pull up the blanket for me?"

Covering his shivering, naked body made me think of my own son and how lucky I was that we were both in good health. It also made me feel a little tender towards this sick stranger. "Can I get you anything else," I asked, suddenly maternal.

"Hmmm," he thought, tucking the blanket under his arms, "maybe a Portuguese boy with long hair and a Vodka martini?" We giggled a bit and I finally managed to get the window open. The room was flooded with light and the sun reflecting off piles of sequins and metal momentarily blinded me. I picked up a bundle and examined it. It was a purse, a really beautiful purse. I wandered where the woman was to whom it belonged. "Wow, what a beautiful purse," I said. The skeletal frame on the bed moved a little to face me.

"Ah, yes. That's my Chanel clutch, one of the design house's first bags released onto the market." He smiled the way a parent would at an overachieving child. I placed it on the dresser with care, since it was obviously important to him. Picking up a few articles of clothing scattered beside the bed, I unearthed three more treasures. Their owner greeted each discovery with a short biography. "That's a Fendi from the eighties, at the height of color decadence. Ah, that one's fairly new. It's a Gucci I picked up in Italy a couple summers ago - Oooo, one of my favorites, a Fortuny piece from the twenties." Soon we had spread the purses out on the bed and he was sitting up telling me about each one and the stories of how he came to own them. They were like signposts on his personal road marking important historical sites.

Now it seemed that he had come to end of his journey. I couldn't help but wonder what would become of those purses I had displayed around the room for him after he had fallen into fitful sleep that afternoon.

Now I wanted to get past these jerks so I could make sure his purses were safe. I cleared my throat and made my way down the hall innocently. "Did I hear that there was a call for extra towels up here?" The three of them turned around as I approached. Night Manager put his arm around my shoulder and steered me away from the doorway. I caught a glimpse of a pair of feet in expensive looking shoes near the end of the still made bed. "Yes, yes, thanks, but, uh, the guest in Room 502 no longer requires any towels."

"Really, did someone already bring them," I questioned, straining to peer into the doorway as Dave, the Maintenance Supervisor shook his head solemnly as if I were a small child missing the point completely. They behaved as though I had interrupted a terribly important meeting with my irrelevant gibberish. I hate Dave.

"Naomi," he spoke gently, not wanting to upset me. He spoke like a police officer who, with hat in hand, had bad news to share at three in the morning. "This guest has met with an unfortunate end. I'm afraid he has passed away." He hung his head and patted my shoulder.

"Oh no," I feigned shock, clutching my warm towels to my chest. "Really, sir? Another one? Well, what do we do now?"

He laughed slightly, "Oh, you don't worry about that, Naomi. Dave and I will handle everything. You just carry on and don't talk to the guests or other staff about anything. We don't want to create a scene, you see. After all, this will be the second death here in a short period. We do need to protect the company, you see."

I nodded stiffly as he guided me back down the hallway towards the elevators. He pushed the down arrow, arm still around my shoulders and smiled. "No foul play here, but still, it just doesn't sit well with people to have a death in the building. You know what I mean."

I nodded, wishing he would take his arm off me. The elevator arrived with a 'ding' and he loaded me on. "Thanks for your understanding, Naomi. You're a super employee." He gave me a weak 'thumbs up' before the doors slid shut.

"Asshole," I muttered, pushing the basement button. I felt like I had missed the opportunity to have a great friend, someone who made me enjoy my job more that I did. Through our visit on that brief afternoon, I came to appreciate that each room was a veritable library of stories, and each guest a curator of sorts. It made me want to stumble upon more occupied rooms and to hear more tales. "Dammit." I needed to find Carlos and his weed before I tried to get through the rest of this doomed shift.

In the story of a death it is better to 'accentuate the positive', to apply an old Avon lady's philosophy. Following this bit of mail-order wisdom then, we can say that this is the story of a life rather than a death. How much can really be told at this late hour, though? I guess it's better to describe the sunrise in the morning, rather than just as you are climbing back into bed, head filled with sordid tales and a bit of whiskey at the very end of the day. Details are lost in the pause.

At the end, he could see death. It lit him a cigarette and propped it between his purple lips. Death never faltered. It tightened its icy grip around his neck. His life jumped on the back of a passing pick-up bound for fruit filled fields and flipped him the bird.

Marcel was born in a small, second-rate hospital in a third-rate city somewhere tragically boring. His mother said that the moment he batted his impossibly long eyelashes at the obstetrician on that snowy February morning thirty-two years ago, she knew he was bound to be the greatest man who ever lived. Clearly the woman had inhaled a little too much gas, but nevertheless, two things were abundantly clear; his mother had faith in him and he was blessed with killer eyelashes. Both would serve him well.

Marcel's first memory appears as a traumatic blip at age four. He favoured a pair of beige flannel PJs. They were a gift from his favourite Auntie the previous Christmas and, thanks to a Cheerio's-powered growth spurt, they pulled away from his ankles and wrists as if recoiling in wrinkled disgust. He wore them everywhere and they were covered with the decidedly un-bedtime stains of grass, mustard, Coke and tomato sauce. They were a white trash mosaic.

So, there he was, crouched in the space under the sink, next to the leaky pipes tied with bits of old rag and duct tape in vain attempts to prevent the steady dripping, playing with his G.I. Joe action figure. There was a frayed towel hanging where a wooden door had rotted off, separating the damp cubby from the rest of the kitchen.

G.I. Joe was dodging in and around Javex and blue window cleaner bottles, desperately seeking his long-time companion, Snake Eyes, who had been captured and carried off by evil Amazon Women on the Moon (played by his sister's Barbies, all of whom had received choppy, uneven 'dos that revealed their hair plugs, making them resemble middle aged car salesmen). He would yell this last part loudly in a baritone as if it were an old-time movie title. He never had a Snake Eyes figure. He would have to wait until his next birthday and do a whole lot of whining for that. So, Joe was forever mourning the absence of his main man and searching for him high and low, like so many tragic stories. Sometimes

Joe heard Snake Eyes moaning in an injured way, but inevitably, the Amazon Women on the Moon would grab him up and tie him down. He would then be subjected to all kinds of inhumane tortures that would kill a lesser man. He always escaped, but his shirt never made it out in one piece and he would brave the next adventure all pecs and abs, hoping to run into his mangled clothing dangling from a tree or stuck under a spongy rock.

Joe managed to escape his dreaded enemies and was hiding high up on the sweating pipe when the side door banged open. Little Marcel looked out from around the towel. The water that had been running steadily as his mother finished the lunch dishes was shut off. Light flooded the kitchen and he saw heavy work boots making their way across the linoleum. He didn't recognize these boots. His father didn't need work boots since he didn't work. And besides, he had gone up north hunting and wouldn't be back until the weekend. Today was only Wednesday. Marcel stayed perfectly still, feeling a strange sense of immobility and something akin to fear.

The man stood behind Marcel's mother. Marcel saw her sturdy legs, in their dark beige pantyhose, in front of the kitchen sink. The man's dirty jeans pressed up against her legs. He heard muffled voices and lilting laughter, a sound that fascinated him as it was so rare in this house. Marcel's anxiety over having a stranger in the house disappeared with his mother's laughter. The laughter had deep medicinal properties that made him want to jump out of his cubby like a pajamaed super hero and start jigging around the kitchen, singing the Orange Blossom Special at the top of his lungs. Marcel wondered what the man would do if some strange little kid in dirty pj's threw open the towel in front of him and skipped and twirled around the kitchen table. He pictured being kicked at with those heavy boots while the man swore in surprise, so he stayed put.

His mother was saying, "Stop it," in a way that Marcel recognized from when his father tickled her and which clearly meant, "Don't stop it." Then she and the man, still clinging together in this familial embrace, backed away from the sink. He saw his mother's face now, looking up into the man's face, his flannel checkered back to the boy. Her eyes were wide and bright. She wiped her forehead with the back of her hand, still wet from the dishwater, and at that same moment the man leaned in and kissed her full on the mouth.

Marcel never saw his parents kiss or carry on like this, so he was confused. She pushed him away playfully at first and then her eyes darkened and gained a heavy quality usually associated with the kind of end-of-day tiredness that warned her kids to quit jumping around the living room unless they wanted a good smack on the ass. "Watch out," Marcel wanted to yell out to the man, "she's gettin' tired and if you don't quit buggin' her for a kiss you're going to get a good smack on the ass!"

But instead, she pulled him back to her and, leaning back on the plastic of the kitchen table-top designed to resemble wood panelling, she wrapped her legs around his waist. Marcel covered G.I. Joe's eyes as the man's calloused hands ran up his mother's legs. He could hear the rough skin catching and grating on her cheap nylons. He heard his mother's soft moans and a zipper being ripped down. The rickety old table squeaked and shimmied in protest. Then he ducked back under the sink and tried to climb up into the joints of the sweaty pipes.

His mother found him under the sink two hours later after the man had left. She had taken a bath and, noticing him missing, she ran through the house screaming frantically. Marcel listened to her call but felt that to come out of hiding and into real time would be too harsh. Emerging from darkness and into the sun would be too much of a change for him to bear. He stayed in the darkness for so long he saw black and blue spots before his eyes for hours afterwards and no amount of cookies and cold milk provided courtesy of his mother's guilt could erase them.

Marcel's elementary school was ugly. The building itself had been slapped together in 1954. It had only one floor and for some reason, it was felt that in order to look official and institutional, it must have garish green metal doors and window panes. It was reminiscent of snot and prisons.

There was a flagpole out front that was meant to inspire pride and patriotism. Unfortunately, with its rusty metal and the raggedly faded pink leaf of the Canadian flag that flew from it, all it did was inspire kids to play the odd winter 'tongue to the pole' game. After watching Aaron Daniels rip the entire layer of skin off his tongue in a blind panic to detach himself one year, Marcel himself was never tempted to try it. The flap of skin stayed there all winter and each morning a group of curious onlookers who had heard the tale would gather round and nod solemnly after inspecting the pole.

No matter how hard the groundskeeper, Mr. McGregor, tried each and every spring to coax grass out of the dusty earth, there was never anything but scrub and weeds that pushed their way through the front lawn area. The back-fields were not much better. You were just as likely to get yellow dandelion stains on the knees of your rugby pants as the green grassy kind. It wasn't a full size field anyway.

Marcel didn't remember much about the lower grades other than the paste tasted really bad and having to go out for recess no matter how cold it was. The students would try to hide in the washrooms and even get into trouble so that detention would carry through 'outside time,' but the teachers didn't want to give up coffee and flirting time in the staff lounge, so they started handing out 'in class' detentions instead and the dreaded 'extra homework assignment for the whole class,' punishment that usually got you beat up after school. But he did remember grade five.

Marcel's teacher in grade five was Ms. Cochimilio. She was a tall, slim lady with deeply died blue-black hair. She must have touched up her colour every week because she never quite got rid of that acidy salon scent that hung around her head like a L'Oreal halo. She had huge eyes an odd shade of blue and wore an overwhelming amount of matching eye shadow. Her cheeks seemed cruelly slashed from a distance, as though she'd been tortured with a branding iron in some foreign POW camp defending national secrets, but upon closer inspection, there were just cakey streaks of foundation. She had a fetish for large scale, theatrical jewellery and would never be found without at least two blinding cubic zirconium rings and a couple sparkly necklaces draped across her concave collarbone like some Pirate's booty on a cursed skeleton. In fact, years later when he was in high school, Ms. Cochimilio passed away from some disease that was only spoken of in hushed, small town terminology as 'women's problems.' Marcel left school early on a Wednesday to attend her funeral. When he got there, he made his way up to the casket and stared into the velveteen interior, not really expecting to be shocked or saddened. More than anything he was curious.

And there she was, thinner and less dramatic in a long, flowered dress, without her famous make-up and with only one tasteful ring on her middle, right finger. Marcel burst into quiet but profound sobs that made his nose run onto the fake opulence of her casket. It wasn't that he missed her so incredibly or that they were ever life-alteringly close. He cried because he was touched by the knowledge that this woman died alone, that there was no one who really knew or loved her. Anyone who knew or loved Ms. Cochimilio would never have allowed her to be viewed with no makeup on or without a stunning array of gaudy jewellery. He left before the service began, went home and got stoned behind his garage.

In grade five, when he was ten years old, Marcel took his first steps into the dazzling world of Sex Ed. The kids in his class had heard about it from the older kids and it was talked about a bit by the parents when they came in their various station wagons and minivans after school. They were concerned about the nature of the curriculum. They were worried that their children would be shown pastel, two dimensional shadow pictures of the opposite sex's internal organs and be whipped into a pre-pubescent frenzy that would entail recess make-out sessions, and lead to ten-year-olds covered in hickies sitting at the dinner table and finally to adolescent parents trying desperately to get jobs while living in their parents' basements. Once they were invited to a highly anticipated PTA meeting in which they were supplied all the information and examples of the course materials, their bizarre Roman Polanski inspired fears seemed to subside. They were also told that they had the option of pulling their children out of the class, but no one wanted to look like the fascist Christian parent whose child was too immature to handle a little sexual biology, so everyone stayed.

As for the kids, they didn't really care at all. They all knew what sex was at that point. "Fucking is when you stick your dick into the girl's thingee and wiggle around until stuff spews outta you," Marcel was schooled by twelve-year-old Frederick Murray from across the street in the housing projects where he lived. "Oh yeah, and if you don't pull out in time, you end up with kids, an' then you're stuck with her for the rest of your life. Man, then you pay strippers just to see some titties because once a girl has a baby, she can't do it ever again!" Marcel thought that Frederick Murray's dad was probably a really unhappy man. After that lesson nothing could really shock him, especially nothing Ms. Cochimilio could tell him in her even, level voice.

The first day, Ms. Cochimilio handed out thin workbooks entitled 'Your Body, Your Responsibility'. "Great," Marcel thought as he took one from the top and passed the stack down the rows. "That's just what I need, more responsibility."

He flipped through the book, studying the much feared dia-grams of what appeared to be the Chicago Bull's team logo on the inside of a girl shadow and a growth chart that had 'pubic hair and acne' slotted in for us in the next two years. What fun! They began the lessons without much fanfare and without too much giggling, except when Ryan Thunderbird asked in all earnestness when he was going to get his period.

A few weeks later the class got to reproduction. The diagrams thrown across the white brick wall from the dim projector showed a blue cut-away boy outline lying on top of a pink cut-away girl shadow. They were tied together by a blue ribbon that was intended to be a penis. Ms. Cochimilio explained that 'abstinence is normal and healthy, that sexual development is healthy and natural, and that, as you grow older, there would be many ways to express sexuality." She pointed to the diagram and said, "When you are adult and in committed and loving relationships, this is how you express this love. This, boys and girls, is sex and at some point in your lives, hopefully later rather than sooner, you will experience this love between a man and a woman."

From the back of the room, someone yelled, "Except Marcel. Marcel is a fag." There was much giggling, as though Ryan Thunderbird had asked about when he should expect menopause.

He had never been called a fag before, and it didn't sit right with him, like an itchy sweater that made it hard to breathe. But he didn't fight back, just sank lower into his seat, as though being somewhat shorter would erase him from existence, at least right now and for the rest of this class.

In high school, things were not much better. Not horrible, just forgettable and uninspired. Marcel began to feel like maybe it was a waste to get up in the morning because whenever he did, he spent the day trudging around in a world where nothing made sense. Everything was bleak and monotone. He began to think that he was suffering from clinical depression and decided to seek out the help of a trained professional who could prescribe the right drug that would help him get through his Pop Tart and into the day. The first step was to approach the school guidance counsellor. At his school this was a woman named Miss Fallbrook, who favoured polyester pants and mint scented denture cream.

Miss Fallbrook should have been a gym teacher because she was, (a), useless and (b), so obviously a dyke. As far as being in the closet went, hers was so shallowly disguised it was barely a clothes rack (with a few basketball uniforms hanging from it). But she was the only guidance counsellor and was shared between two schools. And at this point, Marcel was desperate.

So, he waited until Thursday (Tuesdays and Thursdays were their days, Stephen Leacock Collegiate Institute got her Wednesdays and Fridays and the 'special kids' school got her on Mondays), and requested an appointment during morning study hall.

Since she was only part time, Miss Fallbrook didn't actually have an office. Instead, she counselled from, ironically enough, an old supply closet. She talked to spotty-faced nerds and seniors unsure of whether they should go on to community college or just take a 'sweet' gig at the mill with their dad after graduation. She fit right in among the folded up volleyball net and the stacks of mouldy exercise mats, the big lesbian.

They sat there, at 11:00 a.m., her first and only appointment for the day. There was a card table between them and when Marcel leaned on it with his elbows it wobbled on uneven legs. "So," she began. "What can I do for you today?"

He waited for the table to stop wobbling and spoke clearly, almost pleadingly, "I think that I am gay."

This, of course, was a lie. He full out knew that he was gay. But he wanted to leave some room around the title in case Miss Fallbrook had some miraculously simple explanation for the whole, difficult mess: "No, actually Marcel, you're not gay," she would assert. "You just have a bit of mono. Here's a helpful pamphlet all about it and a note to get you back into class." In reality, her face turned bright red and she looked nervous as though instead of saying, "Miss Fallbrook, I think *I'm* gay," he had blurted out with a quivering accusatory finger pointed across the wobbly table, "Miss Fallbrook, I think *you're gay!*"

"Well, um," she stalled, folding and unfolding her hands and shuffling the stack of helpful pamphlets on her makeshift desk. She cleared her throat. "Really? How interesting. Well, why would you think that Marcel? Have those boys been teasing you again?" And then, as if she were on to something, she spoke more calmly and with enthusiasm. "Because you know, just because you're not good at sports, that doesn't make you gay." She stifled a hysterical sounding giggle.

Clearly, the meeting was over. "Yes, yes, you're right Miss Fallbrook. Thank you for your time. I really should be getting to third period." He stood up and grabbed the canvas knapsack that had been lying at his feet.

CRASH!

The card table tumbled to the ground, sending pamphlets flying through the air. The strap of his bag hooked itself around the gimpy table leg. Looking around at the, "So you're body is changing," "Saying no is the most positive thing to do," and "There is no I in Team," brochures on the floor, on the folded net, across Miss Fallbrook's lap, he left and closed the door behind him.

Telling the guidance counsellor had been Marcel's practice run at telling his mother. But he decided mature truth sessions were not the way to go. Instead, he just let her catch him making out with Billy Sierra the next summer.

There is a huge gap here where nothing really stands out. He was incredibly bored. He lived with his mother until he was twenty-six so he could finish graphic design school and because he didn't want to leave the old broad all alone. He was convinced that left alone, she would begin that slow spiral dance into insanity that hits some empty-nesters after their spouses have died from quick paced colon cancer and their children are off living glamorous lives in far away cities. His sister had already moved to Vancouver and was living in some modern loft, writing modern columns for an artsy, and therefore unreadable, magazine.

When he was twenty-six his mother decided to leave him, the crazy old bird, and flew off to stereotypical Orlando with a cousin, to live the rest of her days infused with margaritas in the land of liver spotted beach communes and Wal-Mart dominated strip malls. Whatever, Marcel, once and for all, decided to leave this horrid one-horse town and moved to what he had always referred to in his boring years as, 'the Fabulous City.'

The Fabulous City was expensive, so he moved in with two other people into a tiny-roomed, but well situated apartment right near the best gay clubs and the downtown core where he worked as the in-house designer for a well-known French cosmetics company. They were so pretentious in the office even the air smelled like lavender. Marcel knew that they wouldn't have hired him if he were straight unless he had a thick accent, in which case he would have been one of the Client Liaisons to keep up the well-groomed French image. It was beautiful.

And for the first time, he had community. Growing up Métis, he hadn't really fit in with the kids who were bussed in from the reserve each day or with the white kids in town who threw stones at anyone they deemed different, feminine half-breeds included. So he grew up without community. Now, here he was, sitting on the patios of coffeehouses laughing and flirting; meeting friends for Sunday brunch at the restaurant near his place; dancing and fucking away the weekends. Even the employees at the little bookstore he frequented knew his name and were happy to see him. It was as if the entire neighbourhood was Cheers and Marcel was a slimmer, better looking Norm Peterson. It was the year that he turned twenty-eight that he finally got his own place: a little studio with great views in that same neighbourhood, a little dog with a great personality he named Humper (yes, the name fit even though she was a girl), and it was also the year he met Jack.

The Fabulous City, Marcel soon discovered, had fabulous vintage stores. He spent many Sundays strolling through dusty old shops and snobby antiques stores looking for the pieces that would personalize his studio. He figured there was no better way to find himself than in other people's throwaways.

One humid summer Sunday in particular, he wandered into 'The Curio Cabinet,' a second hand store that specialized in (gasp) couture. Every available inch of the place was covered in sequins, silk, feathers, rhinestones, De La Renta, Chanel, Schiaparelli and even a few treasured House of Worth masterpieces. He touched every hem and fingered all the lace, lost in such exquisite textile sensory. But it was when he had snaked his way through the aisles and to the front register with its glass display cabinets that Marcel really fell in love. Sitting by an old man in a faded denim shirt, glasses perched precariously on the tip of his nose while he read a serious looking book, was a collection of designer handbags. He could never be sure what exactly attracted him, but he could not resist. They looked like candies in different shapes, sizes and flavors and they beckoned to him like musty-smelling hustlers. Oh, and the old guy, that was Jack.

He pulled out each piece that Marcel asked to inspect and they talked about the detailing of the seams and the durability of the hardware clasps. In the end, he purchased a red pleated Chanel for a mere $750, whose only flaw was a few rust stains on the inside lining. This is where his soon to be monumental handbag obsession began and also when he and Jack started down the road to being best friends.

Each weekend he made his way back there knowing that Jack would keep the best prizes at the best prices tucked away in scented tissue paper behind the counter. Sometimes he shopped, or brought preferred friends, and sometimes Marcel just brought lattes and he and Jack stood around talking. As it turns out, Jack was a history buff and his most favourite subject in the entire world was Louis Riel, or as he called him, 'The Unsung Father of Confederation'.

"If this country had to take a paternity test to see who was the daddy: American businessmen, English monarchy or a rebellious Métis who brought about annexation of the West," he was fond of declaring, "the Orange roots of this nation would be shaken to the core." Marcel would roll his eyes, completely uninterested in this CBC sounding drama. This infuriated Jack to no end.

"How can you be a part of such a great history," he would almost scream. "How can you be descended from such nobility and character, be the living embodiment of all that is Canadian and unique, and be so indifferent?" To which Marcel would ask him how he could be owner of such a great little shop and still be such a bitchy old queen. He would sigh and slowly shake his grey head, exasperated by the unwavering apathy.

Not that he didn't try to stir up some great tear-wrenching pride from Marcel, only to get much the same results as that kid with elementary school flag got which was nothing, except a smart mouth. As soon as the little bells would tinkle announcing his friend's arrival in the store, Jack would begin in a loud, steady voice, disembodied and floating over the heads of the Halston clad mannequins like a less interesting version of Vincent Price, *"To secure their demands, the Métis called upon Riel to lead them in establishing a provisional government and drawing up a petition of rights. Riel succeeded in empowering and protecting his people. He negotiated the Manitoba Act of 1870, which incorporated many of the Métis demands such as language rights, denominational schools and land grants. Riel was able to accomplish the objectives of the Métis because of his knowledge of the legal and constitutional process. As a result of Riel's efforts, it was recognized in the Manitoba Act that the Métis had an interest in the land which had to be extinguished before the government could lay claim to it."*

And this is where he would get even louder and bossier sounding. *"And, because Riel negotiated the terms upon which the Settlement entered into Canada as a province, he should be recognized as the "Founder of Manitoba" and a "Father of Confederation."*

Marcel would mimic his words and throw hands up to cheeks with mock surprise and amazement. "Yes, yes, you can make fun," he would scold. "But you should know this stuff, missy. It's important stuff."

Two years and twenty-four handbags later, Jack's HIV had progressed and he was dying of AIDS related pneumonia.

Marcel went over to Jack's townhouse every day, picking up Humper from home on the way. He and the dog would both curl up on the crisp, Provencal expanse of Jack's bed and watch with big eyes as the palliative care nurses went about their finicky business of changing IV drips and tending to the vials and mixtures of painkillers and anti-inflammatories that lined his bedside table like multicolored soldiers on a hopeless battlefield. Jack would absent-mindedly stroke them both while they fiddled with his tubes and wires and took his temperature every hour on the hour.

It was during the second week, after Marcel had prattled on and on forever with all the usual gossip (who was sleeping with whom, who hated whom in the office, what other shopkeepers were selling fakes and rip-offs, etc.) that he finally noticed Jacks' library. He was unsure of how he couldn't have noticed it before, since shelves and shelves of serious looking books were wrapped around the room like a literary scarf.

Jack's eyes changed when he pulled down a profile of Riel's life and death. Then settling at his feet beside Humper, who was snoring rudely in her unrefined Boston Terrier way, Marcel began to read aloud from the introduction.

"Louis David Riel was a man unlike any other. Born into a Métis family and educated in a religious school far away form his siblings in the big city of Montreal, Louis grew into a well educated, politically aware and sensitive young man."

He looked up to see a smile from beneath the mask and joked. "I dunno Jack, my gay-dar is going off a bit…sensitive young man indeed."

"In this time, Rupert's Land had been earmarked to act as the receptacle for the westward push of settlers that had packed up their bags and headed out to this new land. Except this wasn't new land. It was old, very old.

The story of Riel is the story of a people rendered invisible by law, victims of greed and colonization. This is the story of poverty and racism, a story about the people who, through many adversities, held together as a nation and produced a man who would be elected to the Canadian Legislature 5 times, though he could never claim his seat with a large bounty on his head."

Marcel's throat tightened. He felt a bit foolish for the stinging in his eyes and the hitch in his voice. But Jack was listening intently, so he continued.

"The Métis were predominantly fur traders and trappers. They were the half-breed children of the white men who had travelled across the ocean to seek fame and fortune. They were the children who were raised by their First Nations mothers after their fathers returned to their legal white wives or when they died from exhaustion and disease. These are the people who carved out the Canadian landscape with their voyageur trail and red river carts."

He held the book in his right hand and started rubbing at his collarbone, and up and down his chest with the left. Something was growing there and it made him feel a bit dizzy. He was glad he was already lying on the bed.

"The modern Métis nation thrives as a culturally unique and resilient community though they continue to struggle for recognition. Across the homeland there are large groups of Métis who gather together to celebrate their fallen leader, Louis Riel on November 16, the day that he was hanged for High Treason. They have claimed victory by the very fact that they continue to exist."

He cried and the tears got mixed up into the words. His chest was hurting and he pushed at the pain with his left hand the way you might stick your tongue into an achy part of your gums. Jack cried a bit too, as much as he could bear through the medical clouds that hovered around him like gnats. Marcel finally got it and the ongoing argument over his mocking indifference had ended. He read until Jack fell asleep, his thinned out face covered by what seemed to be an extra large oxygen mask. Then Humper and her master started out for home.

It was nearly fall and the air was cold and refreshing. Breathing felt like eating fruit; sweet and nourishing. Marcel walked past the gardens and terraces of this upscale neighbourhood determined to take everything in. How could he take even this flippant moment for granted when his most beautiful friend was slowly deteriorating under false lights and a rubbery mask? How could he complain about men or a raise that hadn't materialized when he was walking and breathing on his own, when his mother was safe and probably drunk in Florida, when his sister had just given birth to her first child, a dark eyed boy she named Biish. Hands in pockets, slightly googly-eyed dog trotting by his side, Marcel walked home and softly cried at the kitchen table for which he had never gotten around to buying more than one chair.

Jack died on a Wednesday. It was rainy, breezy and unusually warm. Leaves that had just begun to change into colorful paper butterflies blew off emaciated branches and stuck to the windows, making stained glass for their own amusement.

They laid there, the three of them, on a red and white toile duvet, watching the weather through the wide balcony doors and listening to the soft music of the oxygen tank, the heart monitor, the shuffle of the nurse's shoes, pills being measured and counted and the wind whispering seductively from outside. Marcel later thought that he should have paid more attention. That he should have wondered at what the wind was trying to coax out there with it into the wet, open sky. Humper started to whine.

Marcel sat up, putting down the slim volume of Riel's poetry he had been reading and looked over at the dog and then over at Jack. Just then the ridges on his heart monitor fell flat like a whole row of silly little drunks stumbling and then passing out at once. The nurse simply shut the machines off and left the room, closing the door behind her.

The music in the room was no longer there. Marcel sat for a few minutes listening for something, waiting for something. And then he noticed that the wind had picked up momentum, that it was whipping about the house now as if the dance had turned dervish and an audience was eagerly watching. "I love you," he remarked, as though casually kissing a partner good bye on your way into the office, breathing in their good scents and heading for the door. Then it was gone. He left.

Jack left Marcel the store and everything in it. He left him all of his books on Canadian history and his precious collection of Riel writings. Marcel sold the shop, keeping only the handbags and a Dior tie that Jack had been in love with. "If I was to ever have somewhere important to go, I would wear that tie right there," he would say, pointing at the thin, gold item that hung in a glass frame above his register. Marcel took it out of its casings and, remembering Ms. Cochimilio, dressed Jack in his best suit and finished him off with the Dior tie. He couldn't imagine his friend having anywhere more important to go than he did now.

With the money from the store he bought out the lease on his studio. He bought matching chairs for his kitchen table, sent his new nephew a good start at a college fund, put Humper in the best day-care money could buy and left for Amsterdam. His work and his life could wait a month while he frolicked and forgot.

Amsterdam was everything that Marcel needed it to be. It was crooked and cobble stoned, intellectual and carnal, beautiful and slutty. Amsterdam was easy, and so was he. He stayed in a colourful five-story house that had been converted into a bed and breakfast, and like most houses in the city, stood on the edge of a canal. He partied and fucked and awoke every morning at 8:00 a.m. regardless of how much he drank, partied and fucked. At eight o'clock he was wide awake, even though he was dying to sleep until Jack disappeared. It was like those spots had returned that had clouded his vision when he was four and had caught his mom doing his Uncle Ronny on the kitchen table. Jack was everywhere he looked and as much as he loved to see him each and every weekend for two years, Marcel hated to see this image of Jack now, his skin as translucent as sliced water chestnut and an oxygen mask that steamed up with every laboured breath.

Marcel sat in the bottom of houseboats and consumed hash brownies. He ate Indonesian food that was so hot his eyes watered and he lost his sense of smell. He smoked hookahs laid out on square silk pillows in rooms down narrow alleyways. He cruised for great looking Dutch boys in crassly named clubs in the Boy's Town of this ancient city. He paid for prostitutes on his American Express and slept with them in Red Light District brothels. He went into crowded vintage stores and bought unusual and obscure purses from tiny old ladies who hardly spoke English.

In one store he paid 300 euros for a thin gold Dior tie, identical to the one Jack was buried with and then after drinking many glasses of red wine, threw it into the canal. Now his friend would be the only one with that tie in the whole entire world. Later Marcel considered that perhaps there were dozens, if not hundreds of these ties in existence around all kinds of necks across numerous continents, but in the heat of the moment it had made perfect sense.

He made it to the Rijks Museum and wept at Rodin's sculptures thinking, "how could a straight man have possibly understood and appreciated the male form that much." He walked along canals to hidden gardens and crumbling old architectural wonders. He toured Anne Frank's House, the floating market, the Tulip Festival, the Van Gogh Museum and Madame Tussaud's Wax Museum. He bought overpriced pancakes in the middle of the day and ate at a restaurant shaped like a child's carousel. He shared pizza with a chubby black cat under an awning on a rainy afternoon. He got as drunk as he could on the free beer at the Heineken Brewery tour. He did everything that one is supposed to do on a trip to Amsterdam, along with all the debauched things he figured he was supposed to do anywhere he went.

He walked under Van Gogh's skies with their overwhelmingly blue tones and huge, striated stars that reached down like phosphorescent fingers. He sat in the middle of an echo-filled room at the gallery, surrounding by some of the greatest art works known to humankind and was filled with their beauty. Wandering though the alleyways of the city that crossed over each other like strings on a cat's cradle game, he heard boisterous voices and was reminded of his own conversations. He was reminded of health and Jack, and their arguments about his apathy for ancestry. Marcel laughed out loud remembering their Odd Couple friendship.

Every day blurred into the next in Amsterdam. Eventually, he could see clearly through his own eyes and he didn't like what he saw. He decided to straighten up, stop inhaling coke and smoking high-grade dope and head home to his apartment and his dog, not to mention his job and friends. But by then the headaches started to come, throbbing at the base of his neck.

A week after he enjoyed a joyful reunion with Humper he unpacked and checked his voice mail. He decided to go see the doctor. He sat in the highbrow waiting room filled with highbrow patients and thumbed through a copy of TIME magazine. He bounced his leg and chewed his thumb. After his dad fell sick and passed away, Marcel's uneasiness about doctors grew until he almost panicked at the thought of having to see one.

It's not that Marcel and his father had a loving or even civil relationship; after all, he barely knew the man. His dad was always out hunting, travelling across the country to visit family or going to pow wows, leaving Uncle Ronny to look after the house and family. But watching a man he thought of as akin to the Incredible Hulk cry and writhe while colon cancer rotted away his guts piece by piece made Marcel fearful.

Sitting on the examining table, his shirt folded neatly beside him, he explained the symptoms that had been festering since Amsterdam. He explained the headaches that sent shooting pains from the top on his neck down his spine and into his pelvis, about the fatigue that made him fall asleep at his desk and stay away from the clubs. He explained that food tasted different and he was starting to have trouble with elucidation. Simple things like colours, patterns and instructions became complex and alien. He sheepishly shared that perhaps there had been too many drugs inhaled, smoked and swallowed but that he had since cut back.

Then he waited patiently while the doctor listened to his heart, felt around his neck and back, looked in his eyes, ordered tests and then sent him to the lab. He had blood taken. He had an ultrasound. He had scarier tests over the next few weeks that ate up whole days and put him in bed while the sun was still setting in a red tinged sky (*"Red sky at night, sailor's delight,"* his friend Charles coaxed from below Marcel's open bedroom window, *"so let's go sailor. First round's on me!"* He got up and shut the window.)

The rest is broken up in a series of vignettes. They were small sketches of the past few months. They were all he cared to remember, really, and in most cases, all that he was awake for.

A word from a doctor's worried face. He noticed that he talked with his hands, and marvelled that his hands could illustrate these ugly, poisonous words.

"Rare form."
"Bone cancer."
"Chrondrosarcoma."
"Embedded cancer in the cartilage of your bones … pretty widespread … pelvic region, shoulders, upper arms and legs, the most dangerous at the base of the skull."
"Radiation. Chemotherapy. Stereotactic radio surgery."
"A year, maybe. With treatment."
"Hospice, care givers, family."

Marcel ignored all the pleas for aggressive therapies. He couldn't be bothered to call his mom in off the beach and into a black corner of depression. Was he to call his sister and say, "Hey sis, how's the baby? By the way, listen, if you don't have your hands full enough right now, howsabout flying out here to stay with me and change my diapers too?" Fucking forget it.

Instead, he became a man obsessed. He was consumed by two things: cancer and purses. His collection of both grew and took up every available space left in his life: quiet time on the commode, the minutes one spends waiting in line for the bank machine or the bus, even those seconds wasted on blinking were now crammed full of the thoughts and images of couture and carcinogenic cells.

He imagined the cancer that grew inside him was a malevolent fetus. At least imagining the tumors stowed in a chic beaded Roberto Cavelli clutch made him feel more alluring in his illness. He was an old Hollywood starlet rotting away on an autumn beach, blanket tucked around withered legs, a spidery black umbrella over her chaise; all glamour and ennui.

The handbags hung in his apartment like beautifully jewelled scarabs on the walls of a tomb. They made an interesting mural in the living room; were neatly assembled in the hallway the same way some people lined up for family portraits and were thrown haphazardly around the bedroom like a lover's clothes the morning after. Looking at their beauty, he knew that he could never die here because he lived here. He lived happily here more than any other place in his life. He left the studio to his dog walker and good friend Charles, on the condition, of course, that he care for Humper. Marcel wanted him to be able to live here without thinking every breeze was his ghost coming back.

Marcel could not bear the thought of lingering. He remembered the months spent pacing the greyish green hallways of the hospital while his father expired, not unlike a pot of mushroom soup left to slowly curdle like sour gelatin on the stovetop. He remembered visiting his dad after school each day, a task he resented as much as taking out the garbage or scrubbing the toilet. He also remembered the look of relief on his grieving mother's face when the old man finally let go and died in the middle of a Monday night. Marcel didn't want to be a chore for anyone.

Marcel obtained a fatal quantity of heroin through a friend of a friend. He closed up his loft, brought his beloved pet over to Charles' saying he had to go out of town for a week on business, and sighed over his impressive purse collection. In the end he couldn't leave them all and packed up fifteen of his most favourite ones in tissue paper to bring with him to the beige, insignificant hotel. He enjoyed them for a few days as he settled into the room and came to terms with his decision.

It was an overcast afternoon when Marcel dispensed with the messy business of injecting himself with enough dope to kill a man, even the greatest man who ever lived ("Sorry mom," he whispered, teeth clenched around the belt he used to tie off his vein.)

In the last minute, before the drugs packed his consciousness with cotton balls, stopping his thoughts like the trickle from a bloody nose, he imagined that the poor maid, (to whom he left a generous tip on the night stand by way of apology, and possibly to help pay for any therapy that was sure to be in order), would find him after knocking impatiently at the door a few minutes to deliver his requested towels. He imagined her throwing the towels like oversized confetti and running to get the manager. He supposed that then the manager would stifle a scream so as to not disturb the other paying (and still living) guests and call the police. They would come and, together with the coroner, rule out any foul play and notify his next of kin.

He thought, "My mother will drink way too much on the plane up here, hoping that there's some mistake and land with a hangover aggravated by thick blankets of fear and anxiety. She'll wander into the chilly morgue in her too thin Florida blouse with her impossible winter tan and wring her hands before they pull back the sheet for her to identify the body.

"At the funeral, I hope, she will have the common sense to know that I chose my clothes carefully and will bury me this way, in the way that I expired. I will be handsome under the dim lights against the real velvet of my casket while friends and lovers mourn in dramatic ways that will embarrass my family. My collar will be starched to painfully sharp angles. My prized Dolce and Gabbana coat will be impeccably pressed. And the Métis sash, that I found wrapped in layers of scented tissue paper behind Jack's old register *("This is important stuff, missy! Love Jack." the little note card had read)*, will be tied around my waist."

room 106

The Staff here is not allowed to show any individual style other than low-key jewellery—wedding bands and discreet gold crucifixes. We can't even stand out with, god forbid, a hair ribbon or, say, nylons with a pattern in them. As a result, we are a pretty drab looking and surly lot, like private school kids or military personnel.

To add to the sterile feel, we keep our personal effects in grey metal lockers in the basement. Here there are no orders around style other than cleanliness, and so we take decorative liberties with the storage units. I think that there is something both absurd and touching about grown people with a collection of magnetic mirrors and pictures cut out of magazines.

My locker is fairly simple. There is a mirror, a list of important numbers on a large Post-it note (day-care, school, doctor, and mom's cell), a school picture of my son and a black and white photograph I found while cleaning one of the rooms. At first I picked it up intending to turn it in at the front desk in case the owner came back for it. Instead it migrated to my locker and it's now become a permanent fixture there.

In the eight by ten picture there's a little boy in an oversized Toronto Maple Leafs jersey. He's smiling wide, showing three missing teeth on the top of his mouth. His black spiky hair has been both plastered to his forehead with sweat and, in the back, blown up into a halo by the wind. I don't know this kid but I know where he lives. I mean, I don't know the name or exactly where it's located but I can tell by the rocky background and the low scrubby bushes that it's north, way north. The pre-fab building off to the side with the hand painted sign that reads 'Canteen and Changing Rooms,' means it's on the rez. Of course, the stray dogs wandering into the frame are a pretty good hint too.

The jersey is obviously a hand-me-down, probably something he wears every day out of pride and necessity. His left eye has a faint shadow of a bruise forming under it, possibly the result of a wicked check during his last tourney. The stick he holds in his left hand mitten is decorated with stripes of silver duct tape and black hockey tape. The skates strung together and thrown over his shoulder are old school with curved blades and high ankles. I tell people it's my little cousin Travis when they ask; too embarrassed to admit that he's a stranger who makes me both happy and homesick.

I know who took the picture. I saw this photographer wander the lobby, loitering near the brochure rack, observing the other guests like a scientist. Sometimes he would start conversations and a few times he snapped pictures of people while they posed stiffly by the front window, hailed taxis out front or tried to light cigarettes while the wind blew.

He left each day with a black canvas backpack, the kind teenagers use in high school to carry their textbooks, cans of pop and little baggies of weed. It was made distinctive by the patches roughly sewn on to it (Canadian flag, Oka flag, Six Nations, Republic of Congo, Union Jack, Australian flag, among others) and by the numerous flight tags still dangling from the top handle. I was a little jealous of the bag, since it was better travelled than I was.

This photographer didn't seem like the usual type we got in here, the business travellers, families and single (if even for one night) men. He looked as though he would belong in a hostel in the Parisian countryside or a boutique hotel in the East Village, New York. He didn't seem like the kind of guest we usually got, he seemed more artsy. Still, I guess some people prefer the rooms they stay in to be blank canvases. Some people prefer the hotel to be a clean slate where they can stage intricate productions without distracting details. Maybe he was this minimalist kind of traveller who needed a basic room in order to ignore it in favour of the adventure of the trip itself. Maybe he was just looking for a bed and a bathroom counter clean enough to lay his toothbrush and razor down on. Either way I found myself wondering if he was here to see a girlfriend or whether he had a wife back home.

I created his story from the picture of the hockey player and an article I found on the computer about his work and life. His personality I pieced together from both steady observation and intuitive guesswork. I savoured this story when I was by myself, making beds or smoking out the side of the hotel, facing the camera shop across the street. And even if his story is only true for me, I still hope he walks back in some day with his black canvas bag covered in a few new patches.

At twelve-years-old the Photographer was a precocious boy who smoked cigarettes and dreamed of mist-covered continents far away from his arid home. When he was fourteen, he convinced his second cousin Brenda to go down on him and then spent the next five years trying to work his charms on every unrelated and available girl on his reserve. At nineteen he moved far away to a city whose lights flashed like fish scales in a pool of clear water at the end of a dusty strip of road. There he disappeared like a sock in a dryer.

He worked at a copy shop xeroxing himself into hypnotic states, punctuated only by the intermittent smoking of many cigarettes. When he worked here he was not referred to as the Photographer, as he is now. He was simply, 'Copy Boy', which at best put him in the running for being the Photographer's trusty, if slightly underachieving, sidekick. His special skills included an expansive vocabulary of various weights of paper, ink compositions and fonts, and the ability to direct customers to the precise colour of card or liquid corrector.

He returned to the reserve in summer and on special occasions like funerals and weddings. His first picture-taking gig was thrust upon him through a series of unlikely circumstances that found him Official Photographer at his second cousin Brenda's wedding. She married a local hick everyone referred to simply as Billy, even though his name was Theodore. Billy punched out the original photographer from Select Shots in town after the eager shutterbug took certain 'select shots' of his bride-to-be while he was away at The Northwest Truck Driving School.

"Lookin' good Mr. Photographer, *aaaay*," his relatives said, clapping him on the back. A borrowed Nikon F1 Series hung around his neck by a rubbery purple strap while disposable quick snaps nestled in each pocket of his borrowed blue jacket. The equipment made him a camera commando, a veritable celluloid gunslinger. *"Watch out! I'll capture your precious moments, all right, right between the eyes! Fastest lens in all Cree country."*

His Kokum curled her short hair especially for this day and wore a giant plastic lily pinned to the front of her special occasion SAAN dress. He bent the wiry leaves a bit so they didn't cover her lower face before taking a shot of her with the bride and groom. She smirked at his perfectionism and pointed at his camera, "Ever good, you. Look real professional with that fancy machine there."

She had demon red eyes in the finished picture but Kokum hung it up on her warped living room wall anyways because her grandson, the Photographer, had taken it.

And this is how he came about his nickname, all because of a wedding where he had spent six consecutive hours watching his family getting progressively drunker and hoping that Billy didn't find out about the whole 'head in the laundry room' incident of 2001.

The summer he turned twenty-three, while still financed by his Band to take film and photography courses at college, he became interested in far off continents once more. The Photographer checked out a book from the library that discussed at length the art of tribal markings and traditional customs of indigenous people from every corner of the globe. He took it home and masturbated over the nudie shots in the 'Contemporary Tattooing from Around the World' section, where women of all races and breast sizes took off their clothes and showed huge menacing tigers or softly cross-eyed unicorns slashing and prancing across their backs and thighs.

When the book was overdue and an annoyed librarian called, he fished it out from under his bed and spent a bored Sunday afternoon flipping through it. He sat up against the headboard and lit a cigarette.

He opened it on a section called 'Mark of Civilization' and read: *The Baule people of the African Ivory Coast have been researched and documented through numerous anthropological studies over the years due to their fascinating customs and traditions around scarification.* "Jesus", he thought, "and I imagined I was a bad ass for getting my ear pierced." He continued reading.

"Up into 1930, Baule women were known for their extensive and dedicated markings that could extend across entire torsos. Today, it is generally only the older women who still bear the markings of this practice."

Pictures of Baule Elders with tubular breasts and serious but beautiful faces stared out at him with black and white intensity. Perhaps the most attractive aspect of these photos was the scarifications themselves; simple cuts that ornamented smooth and wrinkled skin alike.

"Scars known as Nzima usually took the form of a cross and, on the opposite cheek, two horizontal lines. Baule also marked their children to dissuade death from taking them, especially after the deaths of several other babies born to the same mother. It was often a fine line between what was considered to increase value and beauty and what was considered to decrease it and make the person less desirable to unseen forces. All in all, the entire custom required strong belief in the values of the community and its distinct identity."

And so it was then—quite by accident—as he was smoking a cigarette in his unmade bed and reading a late library book that the Photographer stumbled into the biggest question of his young life.

Shit, marking your face took some serious guts, like the refugee Burmese ladies who stretched out their necks with brass coils and survived by selling self-portraits to Thai tourists. He couldn't even commit to a tattoo somewhere in the shirt-wearing region, or even on his ass. How could these women make such a long-term commitment? He reread the passage.

"All in all, the entire custom requires strong belief in the values of the community and its distinct identity." What the hell was a community's distinct identity? Certainly each group of people had their own unique qualities and peculiarities that made them different from each other, like snowflakes or Cabbage Patch Kids. But was identity based on the quality of one group as different from another? He wished he had cable TV so he could seek out the answer to his esoteric question. He believed cable with its easily digestible educational channels held the answers to all his esoteric questions.

Cable was for him an electronic Holy Grail, a divine resource cathedral open 24-7. Unfortunately, the landlord had disassembled his pirated system some months before.

The Photographer didn't enjoy sitting and grappling with life's tough questions in his small, clammy basement apartment while the lady upstairs 'Sweated to the Oldies' directly above his head. But he couldn't stop. He figured that perhaps the Baule were one of the few who understood what identity meant. I mean, shit, they carved it into them, didn't they? They stayed in a back corner of his head over the months and years to come.

After he was finished with photography school, he framed up his Bachelor of Fine Arts Degree and mailed it back to his Kokum for her crooked old wall of fame. He decided it was time to make a trek to the Ivory Coast.

Having made his decision to leave the continent much in the same manner he would arbitrarily decide to run out for a Snickers bar at three in the morning, the Photographer was surprisingly well prepared. His uncle, who had made some good coin by both investing in the stock market and by marrying an old lady from one of those oil-rich reserves, had kitted him out upon graduation. He received a Canon EOS 1D Mark II and a telephoto lens with all the sweet toys to go with it. He also managed to inadvertently schedule a check up with his doctor two weeks before departing and had casually mentioned his trip, to which he was promptly rewarded with shots for hepatitis A, yellow fever, hepatitis B, tetanus, pertussis and influenza.

With a contact in the Baule community secured via email through an international photographers' association, a Lonely Planets Travel Guide to the Ivory Coast and a loose idea that perhaps an epiphany, if not death by mosquito, was waiting for him out there, the Photographer boarded a plane.

At the airport on the other side of the world he thought the humidity that choked the air from his lungs was exhaust from the planes. Going through customs it was his passport and not his status card that showed his identity. He never felt more Canadian than he did in Africa. He hired a cab and drove into town. As he stood outside the car and peeled off unfamiliar bills to pay the driver, he realized that the stifling air was not the waste from the huge engines, but the early morning African heat that would only get worse as the sun continued to rise.

That afternoon he hooked up with his guide, a short fellow named Kweku, who wore a vintage Montreal Canadians jersey, even with the extreme temperatures. He took the Photographer to a Baule marketplace after some strong coffee. The caffeine sped up Kweku's already rapid fire, Baule French-accented English. He was hard to understand. The open-air market was set up in a square surrounded by crumbling buildings, and beyond that, dry, open fields. It was hectic with its makeshift stalls, bins of maize and yams, metal crafts and over-priced masks marketed to tourists searching for genuine Baule artifacts.

The market was operated by women with smooth foreheads and braided hair. They competed for customers, shouting out prices and waving their long arms over open baskets of goods. Kweku chatted and flirted with the merchants, asking several if the Photographer could take their picture. Most of them consented, but a few shied away, covering their faces with calloused hands or silky scarves. Several bore the scars that lured the Canadian across the ocean to begin with. They were older women with serious eyes and strong voices. They allowed him to take their picture without giggling or slouching away with unease and modesty.

Kweku was turning out to be a great companion. He spent hours talking about his huge family and laughing at his own jokes. He shared the more serious stories of his community's history as the two men sat down to lunch at a café half way down a narrow side street. He spoke of a Queen, Aura Poku, who led the people from Ghana to this settlement three hundred years previous. "This is how the people received their name. She had to sacrifice a son to get over the river. Bauh means 'the son is dead'." He chewed his chicken thoughtfully, "We are named for the tragedy that brought about our survival. How can we not continue to live here in our ways? How's that for a mother's guilt trip! She teaches us, boy." He laughed from his belly and shook his round head.

Kweku's stories reminded the Photographer of the old people back home and how they spoke of events as if they were both a million years ago and just yesterday, relying on the cycles they witness all around instead of calendars or dates.

The Photographer spent three months with Kweku, his wife Catherine and their five children, in a village cluster. Catherine did not speak English but communicated with him through an elementary sign language when Kweku wasn't around. She was constantly moving, the hibiscus flowers printed on her skirts blurry in her motion. She bathed the children, cooked the food, cleaned the house, washed the clothes and readied bundles of her yams for the marketplace every fourth day. Catherine carved out the heavy-breasted, strong-calved wooden statues Baule women were famous for. She smiled at her husband when he came home from work and gently chastised him if he and the Photographer stumbled in too late smelling of beer and grease. She and her friends, with their colourful, whirling skirts and plaited hair (the ones who carried baskets of fruits and handicrafts, who laughed easily as if there wasn't always more work than time) kept the cycles of this place in motion.

After a while, the Photographer missed his Kokum and all his cousins—even the ones that mooched too much. The homesickness really set in after Kweku brought him to an old woman's house. He introduced her as his Great Aunt Hughena, a name she had been given by an eccentric Scottish explorer she cooked for sixty years ago. She had an older tribal name, Awotwi, the eighth girl born to her parents and the first one to survive infancy. No one used Awotwi anymore. Hughena's house was a spotless one-room affair with a solid wooden table surrounded by benches. Her kitchen counter was a discarded wooden door propped up by trestles with a wash bin cut into the end. She had an old gas stove against the back wall and a hideously flowered couch against the other. Behind the couch, on the cement wall was a mosaic of photos, some in plastic frames and others taped up alone their curling edges and surfaces yellowing.

After they shared a cup of tea and talked a bit, the Photographer walked over to the couch and leaned in to examine the African woman's own wall of fame. Hughena shuffled over to stand beside him as he looked at each photo carefully.

She pointed one gnarled finger to a framed photo of a young boy with shiny dark skin and two missing front teeth. She spoke in musical tones; Kweku who sat on the couch sipping his tea out of a thick ceramic mug translated. He was doing a half assed job, too interested in listening to the soccer match on Hughena's old transistor radio. It took him a moment to regain composure after the Cameroon team scored. "That is the youngest of her great grandchildren," he managed, wiping at the tea he had split down the front of his shirt in his excitement. "He goes to kindergarten in the next community over."

The old woman smiled up into the Photographer's face in the pause while he waited for Kweku's translation. She continued on only after he understood what she was saying and nodded his interest. She straightened the curled edge of an old black and white photo and explained that it was a picture of her husband, a tall thin man with handsome features and strong arms. It was taken before he left to work in the mines many decades ago. He stood with two other men all three of them dressed in long pants and short-sleeve button up shirts. They smiled broadly and hung arms around each other's shoulders. Here Kweku piped up, "They were driven to the mines by hunger. Many men went. Many did not return; my father, my uncles, Catherine's grandfather. Everyone lost a cousin or a brother. He," he said, pointing to Hughena's handsome husband, "did return. But the lung sickness took him later."

Hughena pointed to a row of tiny unframed prints, all of them showing different chubby babies, some bald and sleeping, others screaming and dressed in frilly white lace bonnets and dresses. She explained that there were many more babies that had been born to her family but that not all of them had pictures taken. She spent a half hour describing the ones who didn't make it to the wall, trying to include each one who couldn't afford to hang here with the others.

Later, the Photographer gathered together as many of her family members as he could locate with Kweku's help and took a group shot that would hang in the centre of this wall. It would sit behind glass in a gilded frame that he would specifically buy for Hughena.

The days went on and he became comfortable enough to wander about the households of Kweku's friends taking photos. The Baule children teased him. He knew this even though he didn't understand their words. They reminded him of his own nieces and nephews, the way they ran about his feet, tumbling over each other like puppies in the long grass. At night, which came fast and furious in this equatorial climate, he lay on his mat dreaming of his arid home far from this mist-covered continent.

The Photographer returned to his city, landing at four in the morning. He emptied his little apartment before he'd left and he had handed the keys back to the landlord, so he wasn't really in much of a hurry to go anywhere. The sale of his school books, his first Olympus camera and the stereo his uncle had sent him for his birthday had paid for the plane fare to Africa, so there wasn't much left of his possessions. He locked his camera bags in an airport locker and settled into Terminal 3 on a hard backed plastic chair for a rough night's sleep.

The Photographer spent the following day taking public transit into the city where he dropped off his pictures with a buddy, who offered to show them to his agent. Then he hopped a Greyhound, barrelling towards his Kokum's cosy house. He shook off the dust of the Motherland onto her Welcome mat and slept for two days, only waking to eat four bowls of moose stew and five pieces of greasy, warm fry bread.

On the third day, the Photographer was awakened before noon by the bang of the squeaky screen door. In walked a short man with a confident gait who went directly to the fridge and removed a piece of last night's bread. The toothy grin under the wide brim of his fluorescent orange camouflage hat was all that he needed to see to know which one of his many cousins this one was. "Hey Gary," he yawned, scratching at the little lines of precise, raised scars under his heart.

Sleepy eyed, he folded the heavy star blanket Kokum insisted he sleep with when he showed up shivering in the newly shocking North American chill that first night (*"Eh, only the best for my boy the Photographer, surviving the jungle and everything. Holeee."*) Gary sat on the brown corduroy rocking chair in the corner, lit up a smoke and offered him one. "Heard you went to Africa or something," he muttered while lighting a DuMaurier cigarette.

"Yup," the Photographer answered, jumping to be second man on the match. "What's been going on around here?"

"Here," Gary lifted the brim of his hat with his thumb, "Heh, nothing. Nothin at all. Oh, Billy got himself locked up. He threatened that little guy from the photo store in town after Brenda turned up expecting, aaaay." He laughed a bit here and took a long drag. "Billy was at that Truck School so can't be his. Anyways, he went to the store in the middle of the day with his rifle."

"Ho wah," marvelled the Photographer, still hoping the head story stayed buried in with the pile of his Auntie's dirty clothes. His cousin slowly unravelled the tales of the rez over the next hour while they buttered old bread and made mugs of strong tea. It was early, but Kokum was already at church getting ready for the fair they were holding there that afternoon. She was in charge of the crafts table and would preside over the Holy 50/50.

"Hey, you know, if you're gonna be staying home, you should go talk to Brenda's photo guy," Gary spat out between big bites of the chewy bread. He reached into the inside pocket of his jacket and threw a small bag of weed at his cousin.

"Why?" the Photographer asked. He went the sink to rinse out their mugs and search for Kokum's rollies.

"Maybe he can get you a job and all. You're a picture taker. Maybe you can, I dunno, like, be his helper or something," he was immensely proud of this suggestion and even offered to drive him into town after the church fair so he could talk to the photographer from Select Shots.

"No, that's okay though. My agent called and I've got to be back in Toronto for Thursday. Some magazine liked my pictures and they want to meet with me." Now that he had said it out loud, he was actually a little bit pleased with himself. He had been unmoved when Kara had called yesterday from her office and told him about the magazine and a big sponsorship offer based on his photo essay of the Baule. She spoke to him as if he were a little boy with ADD, but at least she did her job.

His inability to match Kara's excitement came from doubt. The Photographer was plagued by doubt, the kind that creeps in and puts your pride in a headlock at times when you should be otherwise overjoyed. It's that doubt that makes you take a close look at your sweet little newborn looking back up at you in its little woollen cap with your own eyes in the delivery room and ask, "Is it mine?" It's the kind of doubt that makes you shrug at a framed BA degree and say, "Well, it isn't a Masters, but it might look okay on the wall."

His doubt grew from the same place that his passion for the trip had. It was the questioning place that still tied him in knots, not having found the answers he needed to understand his own identity. In fact, while the Baule had been solid in the demonstration of community and a strong sense of belief and unity, they could not explain it to him. Even if they tried, Kweku's interpretation skills were dubious at best. They were confident enough with this abstract concept to carve the symbols that were born of it into their flesh. It was a paradox of communally covering the body in order to uncover the individual.

"Oh, okay," Gary shrugged. "Hey, we better get over to the church before we miss the first round of bingo then."

The Photographer packed the joint they would share on their way to the church hall to make the afternoon more tolerable and grabbed his warm parka from the back of the kitchen chair. "S'go then."

"S'go then," his younger cousin echoed before he turned at the door, "Hey Photographer man, what the heck d'you go all the way to Africa for anyways?"

Biting off the tip of the joint and spitting it into the garbage pail, he thought for a second before replying, "So I could try to figure out why I keep coming back to this ole rez."

"Oh," Gary answered, "But that one's easy. I thought it was for Brenda's special talents in the laundry room, aaaaayy!!" then he quickly dodged the fist that came at him. The two tussled with each other and fell out the squeaky screen door, set Kokum's Husky barking like mad and rolled off the front porch in a heap of hysterical laughter.

By the time the Photographer was twenty-nine he had become what was known as 'internationally acclaimed' for his work. The critics said, *"The synaptic tension present in his sharp edged subjects can only be matched by the ease in which he captures them. Truly a genius, the Photographer continues to wow the art world with his all-consuming passion."*

He could now travel with ease, not having to sell stereos and used books to scratch up cash. He had a semi-detached townhouse in the city, bought himself a shiny black pick-up and shared a studio with three other photographers who shot brittle models and varnished fruit for fashion and food magazines respectively. He fixed his Kokum's walls and she was sporting a pretty fancy new pair of Sorel boots. She was almost as pleased with the waterproof, fur trimmed, clompy boots as she was with her grandson. (*"My boy, the Photographer, has all his pictures in those magazines Doctor Napew has in his office there."*) But one of the best perks he had found so far was that, with a house, a truck and a job that sent him all over the world and paid the bills, he didn't really have any problems getting women to go into the laundry room with him.

One day, after a few summers of borrowed complacency, the Photographer packed up his bags and drove his new truck to the rez. He bunked on Kokum's squishy old couch under a heavily sewn Star blanket for a few days and then set off to scratch the community itch that still followed him. He began with Gary's house where he took pictures of his cousin with his gap toothed wife and their twin boys. Gary still had on that same orange camouflage hat and showed every tooth in his mouth with his exaggerated grins. His wife had expanded so much in the three years since they had gotten hitched that her voluminous behind now covered well over half the space in the front seat of their truck. But the look on Gary's face when he had his arm thrown around the rolls of her shoulders cast no doubt on his devotion, nor did the look of awe in his eyes in the next frame where she held him clean off the ground in a monstrous bear hug.

The Photographer made his way around the rez and after snapping a few pictures of Kokum while she made bread and protested loudly that she 'didn't have her best handkerchief on,' he headed out to the neighbouring community. He really had only meant to snap pictures of the Cree people whose territories rambled over these craggy northern lands, but when he was done with that, he shipped the rolls of film back to the studio, sent for more supplies and headed off into the East to visit his third cousin who had married a Mi'kmaq girl and moved to Indian Brook First Nation. From there he made his way north.

In one fly-in community it seemed the entire reserve came out to meet the newcomer and have their picture taken. He saw old grannies paired up with their chubby great grandchildren who asked him shyly to take photos for their own crooked walls of fame. He visited the men who worked the trap lines untouched by time or cable TV. He snapped away as children played ice hockey, teased each other mercilessly and tumbled over snow banks and down dirt roads on their way home for dinner.

One icy night, after one of the games was called off when the single spotlight that hovered above the rink burnt out, the Photographer stopped a boy to talk. His two front teeth were missing. The kid looked like his mom had used a bowl to trim his mop of hair, but his cheeks were rosy and already his eyes were etched with deep lines of laughter. "Hey, kid," he said, each word a puff of smoke in the freezing air, "what's so great about this little rez?"

The kid tilted his head a bit and looked at him through squinted eyes. "I mean," he tried again, "what makes this place a home?"

The Photographer spent a few minutes trying to ply the kid for answers while watching him flick bits of snow up into the air with the end of his stick. Finally, when he asked, "How do you know you belong here?" the kid smiled and ripped off one mitten that was covered with little pills of ice. He dug deep into the back pocket of his faded rugby pants and pulled out an Indian Status Card. He flashed it like a badge and smiled, showing off crooked new teeth pushing through his gums. He turned around to wave as he took off up the road to catch his brothers on their way home to warm bowls of hamburger soup.

That night, the Photographer spent time with a schoolteacher who had stolen his heart. "It's more than a card or a number," she remarked, stretching out across the crochet covers of her bed, "it's about traditions and strength. It's about the fact that we are tied to these lands and the fact that these particular lands don't exist anywhere else in the world. That makes us unique."

"Yeh." He was smoking a cigarette, sitting naked on the couch at the end of the bed. "I suppose."

She smiled slyly and pulled herself to the edge of the bed. She slid her long, long legs open and whispered seductively, "Take a picture of this, baby. It's where it all begins and ends." The Photographer reached to the floor beside him and picked up his camera that the teacher had forgotten was even in the room. He snapped off a couple of frames before she screamed and ran to the bathroom giggling.

Now, here in this room by himself, he looked at her photo, the one of her naked back running towards the bathroom, long hair whipping around as she laughed over her shoulder. Her laughter was part of it. Part of the answer and one of the reasons he would be going back up there as soon as he was done this weekend, to see if maybe she would consider following him back to his town house in the city as his partner.

He checked into one of those chain motels usually found perched outside urban airports like beige gargoyles. He was here for the big pow wow like every other Indian he had come across in the last day and a half. He had already taken pictures at the blues concert last night, stills of laughing friends and smoky faces lingering at the bar. He planned on giving half of his work here this weekend to a couple of Native news agencies –friends he did favours for sometimes.

He paced around the room, straightening chairs and looking out the window at the darkened street. Cabs slid in and out of the front driveway emptying out revellers and picking up hurried travellers with their briefcases and backpacks. He sat in one of the stiff backed chairs and sighed deeply.

In Africa, he had thought of his Kokum as he sat with the grannies there that still carried the scars of their ancestral history. She carried the language, the superstitions, the humour and the history of her own ancestral people on broad shoulders. Even in Africa, amongst the anteaters, the gnats, the scrub brush and the heat, with the Baule and the crocodiles and the lush coast, he could taste Kokum's bread and hear her stories.

"One winter us kids snuck out after the old lady went to bed," she spoke as she and her grandson sat near the wood stove with chipped mugs of strong tea. *"It was real late and we were itchin' to get out 'cause we weren't allowed out that day. Dunno why, maybe we were bad or something. Anyways, we went up to the top of the hill and everything looked real pretty in the moonlight. It snowed that day and us, we were just excited as heck to play in it. So we piled onto the ole toboggan and down we went. Just before we decided to get in before the ole lady woke up, Percy decides he's going down by himself. Well, didn't he slam into a pine half way down."* Right about here she made a loud smacking noise by slapping her leg with her palm.

"So we all run down cause he's not moving. We can see his mittens lying in the snow a few feet from his head and the toboggan's broke, but he ain't moving. We drag him home and by now it's close to dawn. We know she'll be up to get the fire up in the stove so we hide our wet clothes near the back door and put our PJs back on. Percy is still out like a light so we dress him in his PJs and sit him at the table. Little Freddy uses his scarf to tie him to the chair and we stick a toque on him to cover the blood that's all in his hair there." By now the Photographer is giggling at his old grandmother's outlaw behaviour and a bit horrified at her and her sibling's willingness to sacrifice their little brother so they wouldn't get in trouble from their mom.

"She comes in to fix that fire and we're just being as quiet as can be. She looks around the table, sees Percy slumping there over his bowl and keeps getting things ready. We're kicking each other under the table and watching her, waiting for the wrath of god to come for us. But, she just lets us sit there, sweating over our mush, waiting for punishment. When she goes into the outhouse, we all put on our wet clothes and make a run for it to school. Everyone of us catches sick that week." She stubbed out her rolled cigarette and took a few sips of tea before her grandson finally blurted out, *"Well, what happened to Percy?"*

"Oh, Percy," she said. *"He was just fine. The old lady saw everything from the back window. We were screaming so much, she woke up. She just cleaned him up and put him in bed. My auntie came over later to check on him cause she knew about these things. He had an egg on the back of his head and busted his rib but he was just fine. And we all felt so guilty we took turns takin care of him. But we lost our toboggan and we never went out in the night again."* She got up to start the dishes, signifying the end of the storytelling for the night.

The Photographer jumped up suddenly in this boxy room as something began to reveal itself in his slippery, eager mind. He threw one metal suitcase on the bed and snapped it open. He emptied envelope after envelope of black and white copies onto the slick, flowered bedspread. They slid off of each other's glossy surfaces and onto the floor. He was consumed by a fever that made him sweat and mutter under his breath as he tacked up photos onto the greying walls with bits of double-sided tape. When he was done, there was only one missing. He set about turning on lamps and setting tripods and timers.

Sitting now on the chair, surrounded by the portraits of his people, the Photographer took his own picture. The final result was stunning as it hung in galleries around the globe along with the entire work titled, 'Finding Home'. It showed a skinny Cree man with a boyish grin and a bit of a mullet. He was slouched low in an uncomfortable chair, leg crossed over knee in a pair of jeans and a short sleeve button down shirt. His wire-framed glasses were a bit crooked and his smile was huge and full. Around him were the photos he had taken along his journey through Indian country.

Here was an old woman, head covered by a faded flowered scarf. She was wearing three sweaters, one on top of the other. Her fingers were wound together nervously and placed on her lap, holding a cheap plastic rosary, while on her wrists were the faint scars from a failed attempt to take her life at residential school years before.

Here was a young boy, maybe two years old. His belly sat like a little brown pot on the waistband of his shorts. He was standing in a playground in the middle of a field with no grass, eating a popsicle and staring intently into the camera.

Here was a picture of Kokum in her SAAN dress and her new Sorel boots, standing next to her wall of fame, where in the middle sat the degree of her grandson whom she raised from birth. He was the first one to finish high school and go to university. Her face was glowing and her toothless old smile was magnificent. Around her in the background were the MVPs in her life who have made it to this prestigious wall. There was Brenda in her cream coloured wedding dress and a handful of fake roses, Gary and his wife holding hands and smiling like crazy for the camera. There was a sprinkling of blue first place ribbons and even more red seconds and thirds from track and field events and random baseball tournaments, a few hand drawn cartoons sent by a granddaughter and aspiring artist, a couple certificates from community colleges and a half dozen birth announcements. On the far side of the wall, where the newer items were displayed, there were a few newspaper articles about her Photographer grandson, framed up and hanging beside a couple of his photos.

He carries each of these people with him. They are not pieces of a separate whole, they are each in and of themselves perfect, and they are all connected and inside of one another like a set of cedar Babushka dolls.

The Photographer is filled with the urge to run out and mark himself so that everyone can see his true identity, to whom and what he belongs. Instead, he swings down to the pow wow and picks himself up some fry bread.

room 207

"Naomi needs a man." It was stated as fact, not opinion, and my mother told anyone who would listen. In fact, she spent most of her time trying to find this elusive man; at the mall, while grocery shopping, visiting friends, at church, even at her gynecologist's office. It was more of a job for her than working at the Bingo Hall canteen selling double-double coffees and bags of chips. Someone should have been paying her. Certainly not me, since I didn't approve of the endeavour. I did not need a man, no matter how much my mother insisted.

I had men in the past. I even had a child with one of them; a boy I prayed would be nothing like his father, which was likely since the two had never met outside of the hospital that first day. Men complicated things, and besides sex I couldn't see a good use for them. I wasn't ready to declare lifelong celibacy or to even rule out the occasional fantasy in which I was happily married and in love, but I was also a realist. The men I interact with on a daily basis remind me of how rare it is to find a good one.

My apartment is small, a one bedroom down by the beach. I live with my son, our cat and at last count, four mice that have carved out their home in the wainscoting of the front hall. We've named them Marsha, Jan, Cindy and Carol and the cat, a spotted black and white fat ass named Stripes, could care less about them. They subsist on a steady diet of toast crumbs and cat chow and are so secure in Stripes' laziness that they even pop out during the day.

The place never looks like a décor magazine. It is spread with clothes strewn about the rooms, books piled on the floor and mail stacked up by the front door, but it does have its high points. The walls in the living room are bright red with stars painted on the ceiling. We hung saris from Little India in the hallway and we keep a big bowl of fruit on the kitchen table in case one of us ever decides to ward off scurvy and actually eat some. Until then, the different coloured apples are just aesthetically pleasing. The best part about the apartment is that when I unlock the front door, it is exactly the same as when I left it. I answer to no one and no one complains about my pantyhose hanging over the claw foot tub or the mice living in the dining room.

I wasted good years being obsessed by bad people, people who used me for my support, my love and my hardworking nature. I cried over men who didn't know my middle name, men who resented my boy, men who filled my space with their own needs. I refuse to be a shadow to another man's figure, someone who might kick over my stacks of books and evict the tenants from our front hall.

The hotel is a great place to people watch. There are a hundred different stories playing out here at any one time. And, like a bar, we have regulars. There are men who stay in the same room each time they fly in for meetings. There are men who stay with the same women each time they arrive in town, leaving their wives and families behind.

There is one memorable man who stays with us each time business brings him into the city. He wears his long, thick hair in a single braid and is always impeccably dressed in tailored suits and silky ties. He pays with a gold credit card and never leaves the room messy. In fact, after he has checked out and packed all of his personal effects into the trunk of a cab, it is as if he were never there. Only once did I find proof of his existence in the room. Only once did he leave behind something that belonged to him.

I loitered about in the lobby, dusting the plastic ferns and wiping down the nylon covered couches as he checked out. His charismatic swagger and deep, low voice fascinated me. It was not that I was attracted to him, only that there was something terribly magnetic about his confidence. After he oversaw the loading of his luggage into the trunk of an airline limo and had neatly arranged himself in the backseat, I started my rounds. I pushed the maintenance cart down the hallway to his room. Opening the door, the smell of sex and sweat slapped me hard in the face. I noticed it all the more since my bedroom hadn't smelled that way in a few months.

"Dammit," I muttered, putting the master key back in my apron pocket. I gathered up a stack of fresh towels, a handful of little individually wrapped soaps and pushed the vacuum in ahead of me.

I was startled to see someone curled up in the big bed. It was his mistress, and I found her napping, tangled up in the sweaty sheets, a note on the pillow beside her. She was beautiful, her long hair spilling over the side of the bed, her ringless fingers clutching at the edge of the sheet. She resembled one of those little porcelain dolls with big sad eyes and a dimpled chin. She looked fragile and so tiny on the big empty bed.

I never ran into her after that, though I did see her coming or leaving the building a few times. Then she disappeared. I saw the man a few times after she was gone, but he was different now, his confidence has thinned out and his shoulders sagged in the new lightness.

But that day, something about her made me want to smooth back her hair and tuck her in. Something about her reminded me that I never wanted to be this vulnerable. Something about her reminded me of why Naomi does not need a man.

Constance spent months watching him walk out the door. She was used to this view, lying on the bed, looking at his back as he left. Each time she tried to convince herself that it was enough that he had been there, that he had spent a few hours in her arms. She closed her eyes as the door snapped shut behind him and started sorting through the new memories they had just created. They were all that she had.

Sometimes she stayed a little longer, leaning over the edge of the bed with the pad of paper and pencil both monogrammed with the name of this hotel. *"I am a gum wrapper island in an oil puddle ocean. I am Sartre's three o'clock in the afternoon, simultaneously too early and too late for anything."* Then she turned the pencil around and erased all the words.

Where did it all go wrong? Constance knew that somewhere between the rules they drafted and the boundaries they built to keep this relationship distant and manageable was the void that she kept slipping into. She had pushed away the closest people to her while clutching him desperately to her breast—he became her everything in a place where there was already so much, painfully pushing the others aside like wisdom teeth in a crowded mouth.

She was in love with a man who set rules and boundaries. She found her minutes and afternoons eaten up by thoughts of him and the small of his back, the way his hands covered her whole hips and the softness of his bottom lip. She was consumed by his quiet passion and the rough expressions of it. The way his hair fell over her face, neck and stomach when they were locked together. Under it all, under the kisses that went on and on until her stomach knotted up, the way he pulled her as close as he could when she convulsed, under his hard weight, under and around all of this was the void. His void. His nothingness for her. And Constance became nothing. She was nothing corralled by rules and boundaries, like a cloud cut by fencing.

She spent her days waiting for the phone to ring and her nights alone thinking of him. She was on call, always willing to rush to this hotel whenever he was available. She exchanged her pride for passion and hoped that this would be the time that he would start loving her. That he would feel the urge to take care of her and make her real in his world outside this room. She wanted to be important to him for longer than it took them to smooth out tangled sheets and knotted hair. She felt lonely even when she could still feel him inside of her.

Then he did those things that made her feel like maybe this time was for real. He would pull her to his chest and she would sleep there, however briefly, soothed by the intimacy of his body's mechanical humming in a perfectly shaped collarbone hollow.

"Why am I so weak?" she wrote on the letterhead. *"I feel so young. I feel so old. I am a timeless hopelessness that has stuck to these same minutes as I watch them tick by from a corner somewhere. He was supposed to be a distraction from the pain that haunts me in and out of nights and days, a distraction from the dismantling of six years of marriage, the packing and unpacking, the yelling and the weeping, a distraction from the joining together of the tiny fissures that line my heart. Instead, he is the hammer that is dealing it the final blow and I am left in a million pieces on the floor. Each time he gathers me up again and carefully places each piece, another shard is lost under a couch or behind a curtain. Each time we are together I am smaller and smaller. I am so afraid of becoming invisible. I am afraid of becoming the void that I feel dragging on my hemlines and slipping cold skeletal tendrils around my ankles."* Her writing became smaller and smaller, until it ran off the edge of the page.

She felt nothing but emptiness. The moment after he would leave her, she would feel that empty space, like an air bubble in the blood stream careening wildly to the heart, like she was lost somewhere fatally dark. Why did she place so much importance on something that was meant to be so insignificant? Why did she chose to take away so much honour from herself? Then, as if that weren't enough, she would break apart the small spaces left that were hers with 'what ifs' and 'what nows?' In his own words, she was insignificant and far away from his thoughts, so why did she believe his hands and his lips more than the words that they formed and gestured at?

She picked up the pencil again, ripped off the top sheet, and kept writing: *"I need to be away. I need to put myself away on some high celibate shelf, to close the lid on a solitary cedar box, but I feel as if the promise of him is pushing me into the centre, into the place where it throbs and moves, into a place where I cannot stop, for one moment, to breathe or think or to be still. I cannot be still, and the movement is crippling me."*

Constance thought about his wife. This woman was fictional to her, nothing but a creased photograph at the back of his worn smooth wallet. But somehow that wrinkled piece of photographer's paper was strong enough to hold Constance out of his life, to keep her at bay like an electrified fence.

"I am not in his wallet," she thought. *"There is no smiling picture of me taken in a summer dress on some rural road in front of a new home we designed together. I am not there when he reaches for his business card. I am not beaming out at him from some happy shared memory as he pays for the bed that he will share with me."*

She noticed the small things. The way his fingernails were always cut unevenly as if done carelessly in a dimly lit bathroom, though the rest of him remained meticulous. The way his smile became cruel when they started stroking each other through shirts and half shed jackets. The way he stretched out cat-like on the bed after they finished fucking, unashamed of his nudity, the absence of his Armani uniform so carefully picked and professionally pressed, his hair loosened from the silky braided coil that ran down his back like a second spine. She pretended that she was not awed by the beauty of his form and tried to seem aloof as she ran fingers across him.

Every Thursday she bought black fishnets and every Friday that they met here she ripped them open sitting on the floor in front of him. She'd move aside her black panties while sitting there watching him ruin the careful crease in the front of his pants with his growing approval. She would crawl into the space between his legs and rest an elbow on each wide knee while unzipping and unbuttoning, pulling him out with a satisfied moan. She knew that if she waited just a minute, without touching him, just watching, like a voyeur at a curtainless window, that his neck would become weak and his head would fall forward as if in prayer. And she felt like God. She felt power and importance, though she could not always wait out this one excruciating minute.

Constance remembered the first time they met; thunderstorm outside, absolute quiet inside the foyer where she stood. The first time she heard him speak the clouds had already started to gather inside of her. A storm brewed inside her chest. High vaulted ceilings echoed the sounds of shoes and raindrops as they slid off shoulders, strands of hair and the wide, gold band he wore on his left hand. She noticed them all before the drops hit the cold marble floor. He pushed the thick glass doors open as she stood under Byzantine archways and she felt the sky change; the patterns shifted like a sheet twisting on an autumn clothesline.

"Cocktails at the museum," he purred to the short man at his elbow, a man Constance recognized as an East Coast Chief at the middle of a media maelstrom, a man rendered so mediocre by comparison she marvelled at his ability to breathe. "How fucking civilized of us."

And that was it. He swept past her like a commuter in a turnstile without noticing how her chest had split open and fallen onto the floor like so many raindrops. Later on, in the cocktail party among Chinese tombs and champagne glasses, they were introduced and shared small talk, and whiskey. He, the patron of the arts through his national law firm where he advised on Indigenous land claims and she, the curatorial expert on Native artifacts and historical documents—thrown together by business acquaintances who were sure that they had important Native issues to discuss. Somewhere in between the initial handshake and sneaking cigarettes in the restroom hallway, she had lost herself. She was so lost she had to follow him back to his hotel room because there was no sense of where else she should be. Back to this same room, where Constance was captured like Rapunzel without the hair to be rescued by.

In his room, they had polite drinks sitting on the scratchy chairs. She was acutely aware of herself, as if naked from the waist down in a breezy space. It was painful for her to watch his fingers clutch a glass or pull through his hair. She wanted to put them on her breasts, in her mouth, ripping the delicate seams of her panties in his urgency to be inside.

At once she was conversing about the James Bay Cree land deal and imagining herself bent over the glossy surface of the writing desk with him behind her. And then, as she stood up (she didn't know what the feeble intent was for sure, maybe to leave with a sense of finality and composed honour, or maybe just to excuse herself to the washroom to fuss with straps and powders) he was behind her. She felt his breath before she felt his hands, creeping around her hips, holding onto them like a steering wheel, guiding her to the glossy surface of the writing desk. And Constance was ready for him before he even moved lips to neck. That was the first kiss; not sweet or gentle; rather, him sucking gently at the throbbing vein that snaked its way up her throat.

He pulled up her skirt and the final tug that snapped it past the curve of her ass almost sent her over the edge. Biting her own lip she sought his, but they were preoccupied with the sliver of her collarbone that bridged the silk of her blouse and the shadows of her dark hair. She moaned and he pressed up against her, his heartbeat beneath his beltline. She felt like the room was under water. She felt like her ribs were cracking in her excitement. There was urgency all around and inside.

She grabbed at his hair, shaking it loose from the braid someone had carefully plaited and saw the look of boundaries crossed in his eyes. She didn't care. Constance unzipped him and then, his long hair caught in her lipstick, snaking around her damp collarbone, she turned and bent slightly. When he entered her that first time, she knew that this was more than it should have been.

She was her own captor, the capture not really having anything to with him. It was her own hands that tied her up and tied her down. She felt a divine aching in her bondage. Each morning as she crawled out of her solitary bed and made her way to the washroom, she was already walking towards her cell. As she brushed her teeth with tartar control toothpaste and applied cream to her face she was actually sticking a knee directly in the center of her own back and pulling tight the strings of a corset that would hold her in and make it difficult to breath. By the time she was standing at the window looking over her city, drinking thick, sour espresso and pretending to notice the way the sun was making shadow puppets of the hazy morning smog, she was already having difficulty drawing breath, because at this point, she would already be wondering about him.

Constance was hanging over the edge of the bed now. Papers with scratchy pencil writing on them were strewn around the floor. She started to feel crampy and leaned further over the bed to put more pressure on her lower stomach.

She wrote: *"On the subway, I am numb to both the perverts brushing up against me with hard-ons poorly hidden by crinkled newspapers and old ladies with cruel mouths sneering at my dark eyes. I am unaffected by their lives and their perceptions of mine. They bounce off of me like shadfly wings off brick walls."*

At work, she sat uneasily at a desk covered in artifacts and research that used to hold her interest over the lunch hour and into the twilight hours. Now it was just clutter and stress, annoyances that kept her from daydreaming about the way that he kissed the small of her back or licked the underside of her breasts. She tried to look absorbed so no one would ask her anything. She could not really form opinions or shape sentences that did not contain his name. She was a woman possessed. She had become an attachment to somebody else's life.

Tonight, she found herself alone in their hotel room. She was alone because he had to rush home to the wife, because Constance asked him to go to her. His wife was expecting his baby and his pride and concern makes Constance wax maternal even though her womb is hollow. She ached for the child his wife was carrying. It's as though she never noticed children before this one, like she's now defined by the absence of a fetus. She could acutely feel the walls of her empty uterus and sense the uselessness of her monthly cycle pulling her closer to nothing but the moon and loneliness.

Tonight when he walked into the room, something was different. Constance was always reminded that he was married. He would mention her as though his mistress and his wife were somehow friends, as if they somehow knew each other. He spoke of his wife while with another woman, without guilt, the way that some men can. But tonight, Constance felt the wife's presence as if she herself had walked in with her husband. She could almost see the outline of his wife's profile on his chest where she had no doubt lay her head only hours earlier. He probably stroked her soft blonde curls while she was there, listening to his cheating heart confuse and convince her of his fidelity.

Tonight Constance felt as if his wife was there, sitting on the bed beside her, staring into her face with wide, even green eyes. She felt this image clearly, as though she could reach over and tuck a strand of hair behind her ear if she wanted. It felt as if the wife was resting a hand on Constance's shoulder and that somehow she smiled as her husband sat on the opposite side. He reached for Constance and grabbed her leg. His wife gazed at him with such adoration that Constance felt her own admiration for his beauty and power was constructed of cheap tin. She wanted to hate her, this image of the wife that he had dragged in with him and deposited at her side. She wanted to wish her away, to pretend that she didn't notice the charm of her smile, the way she exuded confidence and ease, pulling everything around her into order and peace.

He got up from the bed again, agitated and excited like a nine-year-old on Christmas Eve. Constance watched him pace, smile to himself and pour a drink from the bottle she had thoughtfully put on ice in the wastebasket. She took the opportunity to study his wife's ghost. It sat still enough beside her that she could make out the tiny fissures around her eyes that denoted a lifetime of laughter and comfort. The ghost smiled again and squeezed the woman's shoulder in her delicate hand, a heavy diamond band weighing down one finger. Her golden hair curled gently like Constance's would never do, framing her sweet little face. She noticed her almost invisible eyebrows and eyelashes, so lightly coloured and manicured.

She saw the curve of the wife's breasts, larger than her own, but in a more ample, matronly way. Her hips were narrower too, and her feet were small and tapered like a ballerina or a geisha. She wondered if the freckles that dotted her nose and the back of her neck continued down her back underneath the loose white blouse that billowed around her.

"She's having a baby," he said from somewhere near the window where he stood with his glass and joviality. Constance kept looking at this mirage of the wife and she reached down to her stomach, pulling the blouse tight now, running her palm along the small swell of a tight, round belly. She smiled again, but this one wasn't so sweet. It was more of a triumphant sneer. She was smug and Constance quickly lost her fascination for her freckles and the comfort of her small hands. And then she was gone, faded into the empty bed and beige wallpaper.

He looked out the window at the wet streets and damp pedestrians. Constance was dumbfounded. How could he think that it would be okay to share this news with her like she was one of his buddies? Especially here in this room, where they met to sweat and swear, clutch and groan, where his wife was only supposed to be a folded piece of photo paper in the back of his worn wallet. "We just found out this afternoon. A baby!" He laughed into his glass and the ice there tinkled.

She felt as though she had been punched somewhere red and vulnerable, somewhere without bone or cartilage. The heat moved kinetically, from the center of her chest, spreading out until she had to take off her jacket and lay it beside her in the place where the pale ghost had sat, holding her trophy belly moments before. Constance pretended to be preoccupied by the bits of thread that poked out from around the buttonholes at the front of her pants so she didn't have to answer, or move, or breathe.

She could feel him looking at the top of her head. She slowly drew her eyes up, along the crisp seam of his pants, to the Gucci belt, the tailor-made jacket and monogrammed dress shirt. She saw the red creases on his neck from the sun and very tight ties. And then there was his smile, wide and honest. She realized that after all these months of studying every detail about his face, every expression from sleeping ticks to growing anger, that she had never seen this smile before. It was alien to her and its very appearance made her want to throw something, anything, a vase, a glass, her voice. She stifled a scream.

She attempted to look pleased for him, but the look came out all wrong. She felt it faltering like a weightlifter trying to hoist unbearable weight. Her chin shook, and her lips curled and twisted and eventually fell. She looked away to hide the anguish that coloured her cheeks and made her eyes look panicked. She wanted to run at him and beat the image of his wife's face from his chest with closed fists. She wanted to somehow produce a knife from under the mattress and slice his smile away like a paper doll. Everything was over and he stood here in front of her like a braying jackass in his 1950s domestic glory. Instead, she walked to the bathroom and, barely containing the bile that was creeping up and into her mouth, spat out, "How nice." The words tumbled over her shoulder and fell to the floor in front of him like sharp pieces of broken glass. He stepped over them and managed to cross the oceans that now lay between them and he grabbed her around the waist and lifted her up against him.

"Kwezanz," he mumbled her little nickname sweetly into her neck, "aren't you happy for me? I'm going to be a daddy."

She couldn't believe it. Here she was suspended a few inches off the floor by the man she was in love with, the man who made her ache for him, the man for whom she had built lodges in her heart, and she was supposed to be happy that he was having a baby with someone else. How could he begin to believe for one minute that she would approve, let alone share in his joy?

And then she thought, this wasn't just him having a baby with some woman; this was him building a family with his wife. His docile, stay at home, complacent, white wife. That was unfair, but her mind raced there ahead of her sensibilities. It became so clear to her suddenly and she felt that if he chose to set her down on her own feet right now that she would crumble to the floor.

Constance realized in that moment that she was never going to be his wife. She was good enough to fuck, to soothe his ego and to meet him for drinks when friends, family or work wasn't asking for his time. She was never going to be as important as the baby over which he was already besotted. And from somewhere in the back of her own mind, in a spot that was covered in cobwebs and shadowy memories of herself, a voice whispered, *"And you'll never be the woman he leaves at home when he meets his mistress in a hotel room."*

In spite of the voice, she found herself leaning her head back so that it could rest in the hollow of a perfectly shaped collarbone and smell him. She found her hands creeping up to hold onto the hands that clutched her to him. *"But I love him,"* a weaker but louder voice cried, *"How can this be happening?"*

For just a moment, drugged by the closeness of him and the strength of his grip, Constance managed to convince herself that none of this had ever happened, that it was all a sad daydream. And she softened to his touch. She melted into the ridges, curves and contours that lulled her into complacency.

She blocked everything out: the wrinkled bedspread, the poorly seamed curtains and rough grey carpet, the slow drip from the bathroom sink, the small cakes of embossed soap, each wrapped like tiny presents on the counter beyond his shoulder, and she blocked out the truth. Words and images from only moments before fell away like the crumbly corners of a burnt cake that she was refusing to eat.

And then the emergency came. It built itself out of the materials around her: the room, the man, the denial. It built itself with no conscious direction from her like the mashed potato mountain in "Close Encounters." It built itself up, this screaming, sick emergency as subtle as a twenty foot, blue neon crucifix on the highway. This sudden panic was blowing across her face and into the small hairs of her arms like a breeze full of tiny, vicious needles. It pushed her head up and back. It made her eyes squint and then focus. It made her pull away out of this forgetful place and pick up the crumbs that lay about her feet.

When a person is faced with certain death or the prospect of something too horrid to fully comprehend, they are consumed by something raw and jagged. It maliciously creeps in a sneaky and silent way, like a foot falling asleep or a nighttime cramp slowly tightening its grip on a calf. Spastic muscles, heart pounding in nausea filled temples, a dizzy swagger and a choking that cannot be explained through greedy gulps of air—pure and all encompassing terror just before the floodgates open. Adrenaline, epinephrine, glycogen, cortical and more epinephrine pour in to every cell and follicle as though a little boy in your head has pulled his finger out of the dike.

At that moment, the little boy in her head had been crushed under wave after wave of watery mayhem. It was a big, messy, stabbing emergency and it filled the room around her. She couldn't ignore it. Not here in his arms, not even if she were standing in front of god himself. Panic slipped into her limbs, like arms into sleeves. It was as though death was spilling in through the heating vents of this hotel with its smooth beige complacency and every sense in her body was screaming at her to turn around and look.

Constance stepped back from him and his eyes questioned what he saw on her face. She was panicking, breathing in raw jagged breaths and flushing a deep bloody red. She paced a bit looking around at the curtains and the individually wrapped soaps, looking for something to grab a hold of to stop the world from swaying. Nothing made sense anymore. There was only the panic and the voice.

It was a whisper. It was the same dark and humid drawl that had reassured her that she was never going to be left at home. It stroked the back of her head, near the top of her spine where nerves painfully tumbled over each other like acrobats with broken bones. It smoothed down the fray and whispered, *"You do not need him. He is a luxury you can no longer afford."* And then she snapped her head back as if to push the voice and its silky whisperings off her scalp and onto the floor where she longed to keep the crumbs of their conversation.

"Kwezanz," she heard him calling her. But she kept her face turned away, looking out at the same window from where he made his announcement. She concentrated on the buildings outside, a thousand glowing windows staring back at her like candles in a windless room. She took in the sky with its smudged clouds and dimmed stars. She watched the cars pulling up to the rounded driveway in front, taxis belching out passengers in untidy rows. And then she saw herself, reflected back in the window. She saw a women bent over, clutching at her throat, arm wrapped protectively around her hollow torso, her empty womb. And she hated this version of herself.

He stepped closer behind her and his reflection, too, bounced back in the window. He stood directly behind her now and she saw his glass image melt into her own. And then his breath was on her neck and his voice was in her hair. "Why are you angry? I am still here with you." But he was not. He was invisible, a detached headless voice fused somewhere into her back. Her skin felt tight and full. She wanted to be alone, not in this room, where she still desperately wanted to cling to him, but alone, in herself.

"I can't do this anymore," she said, small at first, like a ripple on a smooth surface, tiny like an insect bite from an apple, then more firmly, as if the sound of her voice had inspired commitment to the thought. "I cannot do this anymore."

He stepped away from her in the window, his image now fuzzy and inconstant, but nevertheless beside her. She looked at him this way, refusing to actually turn and face him. Not yet.

"You can't do what?" His tone was as if talking to a child. Perhaps he was so full of the thoughts of a chubby boy to take hunting or a wily young girl to protect that he couldn't address her as an adult. Or perhaps he thought her sudden detachment and frustration childish. Either way, it annoyed Constance even further.

Anger began to swell like an open wound throbbing in dusty air. It grew out of the tumbling, aching spot at the top of her spine. It grew at the bottom of her throat from where her outrage was born. It came from her fingertips and she had to lace them together so as to not act on their impulse. She could see the red marks around his neck now from streaky sun and starched ties. She imagined other marks there, evenly spaced and small in span, ten of them.

Just as she was turning on a shoeless heel to grab her coat and boots and make for the door so that she could be the one to retreat first, leaving him here to masturbate with the ghost of his wife, the whispered voice picked itself up off the floor and came back to her. *"Stand your ground. You are not this girl anymore."*

And she wasn't. And so she did. She stood her ground. Now facing his true form, arms akimbo, hips straight like a man, she spoke with the voice that had found her, with all of its conviction and calm, not at all like the wretched, sobbing screech she imagined would come. "I cannot stay here for you. In here there is no room for me."

His eyebrows twitched and then knitted themselves together. "What are you talking about?" he almost sneered. "I always make room for you. Look. I'm even here now after finding out about my baby." And she saw that he genuinely believed this, that he was a great martyr for surrendering his precious minutes, made more precious now by a growing fetus buried deep within his marital partner made in their clean, white marital bed. He believed that statues should be erected in his honour like giant phallic monuments commemorating his achievements as the greatest philanderer of the ages. The plaque below a well-suited brass-plated figure would proclaim, "He always made time for all his women."

He felt that his arms were wide enough, that his hands were strong enough, that his conviction of character was dedicated enough to do this, to be a loving husband and a great daddy, a brilliant lawyer and a feared negotiator. He was the man who made Constance ache for a baby, who made her lactate at the very thought of his hunger. And she knew that her capacity was wide enough and her need was strong enough and her conviction of love was dedicated enough that he would never be everything, at least not for her. And she was sad. In this room, she saw that the emergency had not come for her, but for him. Because he was dying from her life, fading away even now as his reflection in the window faded with each step taken backwards towards the bed.

"I need you to go away." she declared each word like foreign objects at the customs desk of their relationship. These words were foreign, picked out of the foggy and difficult forests of somebody else's life. She had lived for this man. The days that she spent away from him she only imagined as filler in between the main scenes of the movie that her life had become. The pivotal scenes always began with his appearance and ended with her lying on the bed, refusing to get up and return to the filler scenes of work and subway riding, teeth brushing and newspaper reading scenes of her wandering down moody streets, over sad puddles wearing unremarkable clothing. She decided that she should live in certain ways, in very photogenic and gothic ways that he could study or chose to fast-forward through from the comfort of his own couch. She had never needed him to go away before. She had always needed him to stay. She needed it so badly now that she would swear that even the muscles of her legs and the veins in her palms cried out for him. She felt them.

He swore softly from the bed and then he switched gears. "Come here," he coaxed, patting the bed beside him, the space where his ghost wife had sat moments before. He managed a slight smile, one that spoke volumes of the fortitude he did not have.

Her knees buckled a bit when the memories of licking, pushing, pulling, grabbing and fumbling washed over her, seeing him there on that bed. She took one step before the voice that had now grown considerably in pitch and volume and reached out to poke her in the small of her back. *"You are not this girl anymore. Stop playing her part."* And then it did something more. It gave her a new memory, one that wiped out the images of melded bodies and torn fishnets.

She was lying in the hollow of a perfectly shaped collarbone, but everything was different somehow. There was sunlight streaming in from an open window. There were the sounds of crows and crickets, and from somewhere nearby, an old lawn mower chewed at long grasses and hit the occasional hard dirt patch. She was relaxed there, not clutching at an arm or looping fingers around a wrist to ensure that the body could not leave unnoticed. She was actually sleeping soundly with a long, softly-downed arm wrapped around her shoulders. With a hand tangled in her hair. Sunlight and peace. The morning was chiseled from an excavated site in her past. Before, when Constance was whole. And she remembered that feeling. It was fleeting and rare and she had forgotten it existed.

The memory had, she was sure, the opposite effect than was intended. Instead of strengthening her, it perforated her loosely gathered forces until she was a jigsaw of a woman, a great mass of hinges and joints waiting to collapse up on into herself... and then she did just that. She folded into an origami girl and sat on the floor, looking up with quizzical and sad eyes with a feeling of complete, if not compacted despair. What the fuck was she doing? She had literally fallen to pieces.

He didn't ask her what she was doing or if she was okay. Instead, he sighed, a long and heavy sigh, that propelled him up off the bed and over to his glass perched on the glossy surface of the writing desk. She remembered watching her breath frost that desk, bent over its shiny façade, exhaling into hot little clouds with each push from behind. It was this thought that brought her now to her knees. She remembered feeling power in that moment. She remembered feeling an odd sort of pride that she could make a man forget about a woman he had promised his love and loyalty to for all eternity. She felt beautiful.

And now, she sat rocking slightly back and forth to the sounds of memories playing in her ears. On her knees, which were quietly absorbing the patterns of harsh industrial-quality carpet, she watched him drink. She watched as though she was on safari and he was some strange animal with something foreign and slightly dangerous looking about his eyes. This, she decided, was the end of the movie she had made of her life.

On her feet now, she spoke once more without hysterics or threats. "I need you to leave me. You do not belong here." He gave a short, hard chuckle into his drink, downed the rest of the amber liquid and replaced the glass without a dramatic thud. There was a definite lack of dramatics in this room right now. It was as if the room was drama-anemic.

"You don't want that," he sneered at her now. "You cry every time I leave here. Don't think I don't know." He was cruel now, his mouth twisted, his steps cocky as he approached. "It doesn't matter how much you pretend to be asleep or quietly weep goodbye." Here he imitated her with sheets pulled up to her chin, scared, little girl eyes looking around, whimpering. "I know that the second I close the door, you cry. You cry because you love me. And you most definitely do not want me to leave."

He reached out and cupped between her legs with fingers made cold from his drink. "You know I belong. I belong *right here*," he squeezed her groin for emphasis. She pulled away from his stranger's grip and stood, a little shaken, in front of the bathroom door. She looked at him, framed by the window, with the shadow of his worried looking wife coiled around his torso like an Egyptian snake. The woman who braided his hair for him each morning he awoke in their comfortable home, like a second spine so that he resembled a man turned inside out. But it wasn't a secondary support. It was in fact the only one, an outward display of her starring role in the puppetry of his movements. And Constance knew that he was nothing without her.

His wife provided him with the strength that he needed to be able to come here and face Constance, to pretend to be man enough to fill her life, to be more than just a dick. If she did not exist—in shared memories, in the back of his wallet, in a newly terra cotta coloured house on a rural road, he would not have the confidence to be here and to imitate, with wooden jerks and mimed expression, a real boy to his Pinocchio truth. She was his Geppetto. She carved him out of the block that had arrived on the doorstep of her life several years ago. And while Constance admired her work, she couldn't see herself playing with dolls for the rest of her life, especially if she would have to play nice and return this one to its poly-wrapped package at the end of the day.

She smiled to and for herself and another expression she hadn't seen in the months of nocturnal study flickered across his smooth face. It was as brief and as significant as the clumsy and chemical moment of conception, and she knew it. She knew now that he was nothing without her, without this other woman, without Constance.

And he knew also. She saw it. Not in his dark, cool eyes. Not in the tight grimace. But in the slight sloping of his shoulders, as though defeat was registered and conceded. She was the reason he could return to his wife and his other life satisfied. The reason he could welcome this new baby without trepidation. Constance was his youth and his spirit of self and independence. She was the one person that kept him from suffocating under his beautifully tailored life.

And so, quietly, as if to follow the themed calm of his orchestrated demise, he picked up his coat and without so much as the scuff of a shoe or the creak of a loosened floorboard, he left. Just like that. And she didn't die.

She looked out the window and tried not to watch his back recede into a bright orange cab. She watched him fold himself like an origami boy into the back seat, a small and barely noticed eclipse. She read his lips as he gave the driver directions. She could see him look up at the window and try to catch her eyes. She looked instead across the street at the crow that had perched itself in a bare tree and who was watching her with his calm, steady gaze.

The room hums as she lies over the edge of the bed. She drops the pencil and it rolls across the floor. What is that noise? Is it the ice machine down the hall? Perhaps the heat has clicked on? It's a white noise that makes her want to do nothing but lie on the bed. She wants to ruin its precise hospital corners. She wants to destroy its mocking perfection, like a dirty finger across the surface of an intricately decorated wedding cake. There are pains in her lower stomach, in the spot where she felt hollow not an hour ago. Her womb is aching, still, even though he has gone. And then she realizes that he is really gone, for good. There will be no more last minute cancellations to the weekend she never unpacks from, no more messages on her cell phone to save and analyze throughout her long, dreary days at a job she used to love. And though he is wrong about the frequency and nature of her tears, she does lie on the bed and cry.

Soon she discovers that the more she cries, the less pain there is. The small, sharply manicured fingers that are scratching away her ovaries as if they were lottery tickets begin to dull as she cries into the pillows and her deeply fragrant hair. She tries to catch the tears in her hands, to save them, as they seem to be composed of such important medicine, and then she cries because she can't hold onto them. They slip through her fingers and onto the carpet—imprinted knees that she pulls up to her chest.

She finishes the bottle of scotch he started and finds herself calm and oddly riotous somewhere near her stomach. She is drunk in an unobtrusive way. She used to get this drunk before. She would wear jeans and pink heels and totter across the tiled floors and carpeted hallways of restaurants and house parties. She remembers laughing with friends and acquaintances. She remembers finding men to sleep with and forget about. She is full and empty with a strange and unobtrusive freedom then.

The dull throb of her organs is subdued by twenty-year-old scotch like a suburban epidural. She can still feel the gaps and wounds that refuse to let her fully appreciate the silence of this room, where even the white noise has mysteriously stopped. She has no real time to stretch out in her own skin, across this bed where she can just barely touch each corner like a well dressed star fish. She only knows that he is gone and that she now has acute pain in her lower back.

Once, after a particularly active weekend four months ago in which two condoms had broken, Constance spent the following Monday at work daydreaming about carrying his child. She had held her stomach, smiled in a far off way as though harbouring a great and wondrous secret, as though she were perhaps the new indigenous Virgin Mary. She spoke in soft tones, refrained from cursing and called people sweet monikers like "hon" and "dear" in true motherly fashion. She also spent hours and hours browsing websites about pregnancy and birth.

It was an educational daydream. She learned that a fetus resembles a slightly compressed grape until about the third month when it starts growing into its cavernous head and developing the limbs and curves that will make it human. She learned that 5% of new moms develop high blood pressure referred to as 'preeclampsia' that can lead to kidney damage. She also learned that labour often begins and grows as strong period-like cramps and lower back pain.

In this room where they conceived of nothing but longing and deceit, she feels her impossible labour gaining momentum. She feels something coming this way, full and swiftly, like a very tall man down a very small corridor. Swelling and contracting on this bed, crying for the loss of him and the loss of the tears she cannot hold onto. Something is coming and she isn't sure if she is ready. The voice, her invisible and capable handed doula cools her brow and speaks closely to her ear, *"Accept it. This too will pass. Rip the band-aid off quickly."*

****

When Constance was twelve, she went to a Catholic junior high in town. She was tall and lanky and her body had just started to manufacture the immature musky odours that made her shower twice a day. Her school, St Francis of Assisi, bussed all the reserve kids in since the community was too small to warrant its own building or teachers. It didn't matter to the kids that they had to leave their houses by 7:30 a.m. when it was still dark and the air was filled with the kind of cold that made it hurt to breathe. Being bussed in meant they got to travel the paved roads into the small city, passing by both of the malls on the way in. Constance imagined driving to those malls by herself in a car that she would buy with money saved from her exciting office job. She would be going to meet friends and flirt with boys who smelt like mint and went to college. The college, along with the local skiing hills, pumped life-blood into the northern community which would have otherwise died out with the mines.

Sitting in her spongy plastic seat with kids wrapped in scarves, hats, mitts and ski jackets until no one could be quite sure of who was sitting beside you–Constance daydreamed. She dreamt of her future based on boys–confident, pretty boys. And every morning while the orange bus drove through the frozen town centre she would read the names of the bars where her future self would hang out on the weekend nights. She would laugh a lot and other girls would get angry and pout as their boyfriends knocked drinks over and bumped into them, careless in their rush to get the chance to speak to Constance. She shone in these daydreams like a solitary star in an inky northern sky.

The French teacher was a wiry man with glasses that were not from the welfare wall at the Hakim Optical. Not like her own. He parted his hair off to the side so that when he bent over the perpetual stacks of paper on his desk a shock of reddish brown hair fell across his forehead and hung before his eyes, making him look like a boy. Constance noticed these things, along with the multi-coloured sweaters he alternated every three days–green, navy blue and ma-roon. She saw that his briefcase was always messy with creased papers, assorted pens, broken pencils and a crinkled brown lunch bag. She knew that he wasn't married because other teachers talked about it. The women called him "Poor John," and brought him home-cooked meals in Tupperware containers they served with smiles in their tight blouses. Constance would glare at them as they passed by her desk, clopping along in minxy shoes, smiling predatory smiles that made Poor John nervous.

His name was Mr. DeVilles and his students sang the national anthem in French at the start of each of his classes. Constance sang loudly, pronouncing each word individually and carefully, pushing the vowels and soft consonants around her mouth like hard candy. Her eyes followed him as he paced up and down the aisles leaning into some kids to make sure they weren't just humming along or butchering the verbs. One morning she was subdued during the anthem, her throat and ears aching with an infection that her little cousin had passed on when she was babysitting him over the weekend. She sang with her chin down and without strength. It was because of this misconstrued display of apathy that Mr. DeVilles leaned into her.

Her heart raced as his shoulder, in its threadbare green sweater, grazed her swelling chest. The touch sent shockwaves down her torso and into her hand-me-down jeans. She was startled and finding it difficult to stand straight and still.

He smiled a bit before moving on. Smiled at her stumbled attempts to sing in unison with the rest of the ragged choir; smiled at her cheeks that were a stained and sore-looking hue; smiled at her bloodless hands as they clutched at her waistband in their nervousness. Her exceptional pronunciation and superb spelling had attracted nothing other than a circled 'A' in greasy red coloured pencil at the top of her thin grey paper. But her fumbling had made him pay attention. She decided that French would now become her most difficult subject instead of her best.

The female teachers continued their cooing and domestic strong-arming, each vying for a spot in his four-poster bed in his inherited two-story Victorian in the good part of town. John grew increasingly non-responsive to their attempts. Constance watched him grow sick of being picked over and babied while she herself turned into his favourite student with her meek inability to conjugate verbs. She became his favourite when she started needing him. (*"J'ai besoin de vous."*)

During class, he would bend over her desk, put a warm open palm on her back and whisper close to her ear, "Good job. You're improving already." And she would smile up into his warm, open face, the smell of Old Spice and Colgate filling her nose. "Yes sir, I think I'm starting to get it. I spend extra time studying at night." She was desperate for his approval. It became more important to her than her mother's sobriety on those days she needed to talk. It became more special than her spot down at the shore where she could escape with a book without her grubby siblings trailing along. It became everything in her tiny universe.

Constance stopped daydreaming about carefree days tooling around the city in her own car. She stopped thinking about the boys who would swoon at the sight of her and follow her around suspended off the ground on clouds of pinkish admiration like that Looney Tunes skunk Pepé Le Pew. Instead, she concentrated on making herself into the kind of girl that needed John. Being needed would bring John closer and that's what she wanted. She wanted him as close as you could be without actually sharing a set of lungs. She wanted his studiousness, his stability and his endless patience. She wanted to live in the good part of town and to be wanted by the man everyone else seemed to want.

Eventually, spring came and with it her thirteenth birthday. That morning she opened a package of brand new beige pantyhose that her mother had purchased a few months back. She had been saving them for a special occasion like today, the day she officially became a teenager. Constance pulled on a red cardigan that no one had handed down to her and a grey pleated kilt. The bus stopped in front of her little brown-shingled house at 7:40 a.m. like usual and she sat beside her best friend Karen. She had made Constance a birthday card, cutting up one of her grandmother's crocheted doilies into a heart shape and gluing it on the front. She got a good slap to the back of the head for it too, so it meant a lot. They hugged and Constance folded the card into the back of her French cahier, the place where she filed all her meaningful papers now.

She fidgeted and twisted in her seat through history and science, anxious to get to John's class. She had spent the past week anticipating this day. She had played it out in her head over and over until a strange heat grew from somewhere near her stomach and flushed her cheeks. She imagined that today John would lean over, close to her ear and whisper, "Très bien. You're doing much better." And she would turn to him, older and more sophisticated in her newly acquired age and whisper back, "Yes, I certainly am John. I've flourished under your care." He would smile his sweet, crooked smile and looking into her eyes he would reply, "There's something different about you today. It's lovely. You're lovely. Why don't you stay after class today so we can talk more?" She would giggle a bit and lean in with a shared intimacy so that grungy Phillip McCabe who sat beside her couldn't overhear. "Yes, there is something different about me. Today I am a teenager and yes, John, I would love to stay after class to talk."

She imagined that when she showed up after the last bell, abandoning her long bus trip home in anticipation of a ride in John's powder blue Ford Fairmount, that he would greet her with flowers in celebration of her momentous birthday. She imagined that he would pull her to him, and holding her tight against his ratty maroon sweater, so tight that she could feel his heart pounding in her own ribcage, he would profess his love.

It would be hard at first, for her mother to accept that she was leaving, but once Mr. DeVilles made the drive out to the rez and met the family, they would love him. They would be overjoyed to know that she would be living with such a sweet, capable man. Her mother would cry and welcome him to the family and her dad would slap him happily on the back, shaking one hand and putting a beer into the other calling him 'son'. She imagined that everything would be beautiful and she would start visiting John in his classroom as his wife instead of as the little girl in the third row who couldn't conjugate 'avoir.' Her heels would click smartly across the tiled floor as she delivered home-cooked meals in matching Tupperware containers while Ms. Heinz and Ms. Lavallie cried loudly by the staff room door.

And indeed, that day in French class, he did lean over her desk to encourage her as usual. Except that she was too scared to turn and stare into his eyes. Instead, she kept her gaze averted and, barely audible, ventured to squeak, "Merci." But instead of walking away to point out Phillip McCabe's errors with a greasy red pencil, he hesitated. And leaning in closer he asked, "Why don't you stay after class for a few minutes? I'd like to discuss something with you." She could almost feel the condensation from his breath sliding down her neck and into her sweater.

Instead of some sophisticated and seductive remark, she simply nodded and grinned into the shadow she had made over her work by curling her arms protectively on the top of the desk.

After class, she asked Karen to tell Ms. Heinz that she would be a bit late for Phys Ed because she had to talk to Mr. DeVilles. Karen, who knew about her friend's not-so-secret feelings, smirked and promised to deliver the message pending a pinky sworn promise to full disclosure on the bus ride home. When the last kid had banged and fumbled their way through the door, Mr. DeVilles closed it. Constance sat in her desk still, too afraid to stand, approach him, or even to breathe loudly.

He walked over and sat at the edge of her desk. Her chin had welded itself to her chest. Her limbs were filled with heavy water dredged up from the bottom of the warmest sea in the Southern Hemisphere that they had studied in geography before Christmas. He reached over and cupped her chin in one hand, pulling it up so that she could do nothing but look directly into his face. Her fingers were folded tightly inwards and together (*"This is the church, this is the steeple, open the doors and here's all the people"*) in front of her and were pushed against his thigh.

She knew what sex was. She had seen numerous movies after midnight on TV and witnessed enough drunken make-out sessions at 'back 40' get-togethers to know what was going on. It was everywhere—clutching, mashing, grasping, loosening and binding up. But understanding that there was music all around her didn't make it any easier to dance. She knew Mr. DeVilles' intent. She saw it both in his eyes and in the front panel of his trousers. He stroked a smooth thumb across her jaw line and slowly, with almost unperceivable movements, brought his head down to meet hers.

"I'm not here. This isn't happening," a voice tapped in Morse Code across the inside of her sweaty brow. *"I'm not here. This isn't happening."*

But she wasn't afraid, not really. This is, after all, what she had wanted. So instead of shrinking away into the uncomfortable formed plastic of her attached desk chair or whimpering like a little girl with a scraped knee on the schoolyard hopscotch, she opened up her fingers (*"here's all the people"*) and placed a hand on his thigh. He faltered a bit, then cleared his throat, so close to her lips that she could hear the scraping sounds his throat made. And then he backed away. Her hand fell to the desktop like a cold, dead thing.

"You'd better get to Phys Ed then," he said quickly as he walked to his own desk at the back of the classroom. She stared at her hand, waiting for it to turn into a little bird and fly away, carrying her brokenness with it. She had stopped being the needy. She had taken her own steps towards him, like a separate and capable mind, like the real woman she imagined a thirteen-year-old should be. She stood slowly, and then, trying to breathe, walk and hold together the sides of her ripped open chest all at the same time, she left. It would be a shame if his fourth period grade five class came in to a clotted, bloody mess all over the floor.

It took her several weeks of recovering from quick-set springtime bronchitis at home, in her quilted bed (with bratty brothers jumping all over her) to be okay. When she got back to school, everything was less sharp and less meaningful. Math was just math. French was just French. A look was just a look. She got a 'B' in John DeVilles' class that year. She didn't complain. She had lost far more than her 'A' average.

****

Now here in this hotel room, alone, with a slow dribble of scotch pooling into the hollow of her perfectly shaped collarbone, a voice taps Morse Code into her womb and she mutters, *"I am not here. This isn't happening."*

Something is pushing aside organs to make way for its entrance. She's drunk and she's in labour. Skirt hitched up around hips, tears slipping unaccounted for across the bridge of her nose and onto the bed, she waits.

What comes next isn't bloody or pulpy; it isn't the emergency. What comes is like this; first, there is a pressure that makes her breath leak out every pore, a tightening about her heart that makes it difficult to think, a chill that seems to freeze and snap every vein in her head. She curls up into herself, each appendage folding over the other like fingers in a locked grip. And then she has an undeniable urge to stretch out as far and wide as she can. Her feet push the folded extra blanket at the bottom of the bed off and onto the floor. Her hands grab onto the posts and pull until the bed creaks and moans. She opens her eyes and sees the crow, sitting on the window ledge now, staring in at the girl on the tear-damp bed. He turns his head, watching, and then flies away.

Laughter erupts from her womb–her hollow, empty womb–and spills out over her lips. It pours out like an artery had been slit.

It covered the pillows and slid beneath the bed. She laughs for Mr. DeVilles' weakness, she laughs for her foolishness over such a confounded little man. She laughs over this day when she feels that she will die, crumbled up like a failed quiz under the watchful, wistful eyes of a ghostly wife and a narcissistic man. A man who is just one of the failed quizzes in her very long life. She laughs until the walls shake and plaster falls from the ceiling. She laughs until she is empty. She laughs until she is full. She laughs until she is herself again.

This time, she does not have to work at breathing, walking and holding her split chest. This time, she calmly fixes her skirt, slips into her favourite boots and even manages to smooth down wayward hair from her creased but still beautiful face. Standing at the door, she whispers in a voice that until now only existed on the inside, and around the days of her youth. It whispers because it no longer has to shout, because she is finally listening. *"I'm not here. This isn't happening."*

Her back disappears behind the wooden door like a sliced moon slipping away and into the inky night sky.

room 304

Sometimes the most unlikely people wield the most power. They effect change and manipulate fate, even if they don't know they're doing it at the time.

A young family checked out after last year's Native Festival and I was sent in to clean. There were Animal Cracker crumbs in the bathroom, a soother behind the headboard of the twin-sized bed and a few pieces of Lego jammed in the mini fridge. Since there were children staying here and they tend to get into everything, I double-checked the entire room. I opened each drawer looking for grimy surprises. I found a smooshed Oreo in one, a couple of loose beads in another and a book in the last.

At first I thought that someone had left a Bible. Since, like many hotels, we no longer stock Bibles, Christian crusaders sometimes leave their own copies. I picked up the book and was surprised to find it was a diary. Even though I would kill someone for reading my personal stuff I flipped through the smooth worn pages filled with row after row of neat blue letters. It is hard to believe that anyone could forget such an important thing as a journal; nevertheless, here it was.

Distracted by the diary it took me two hours to clean Room 304. I felt like an interloper in someone's bedroom even though this bedroom had different occupants each night. I skimmed the book and then decided to return it to its drawer. I just didn't know what else to do with such an odd thing.

Downstairs in the staff room I snacked on the homemade apple pie Maria brought in for everyone. "Hey, what's the weirdest thing you guys have ever found in a room?" The question was greeted by laughter from all around the table. I watched as Justin, Maria, Rosa and Tina all rolled their eyes and started recounting the strange booty they collected over the years.

Tina once found five hundred dollars in cash. But that wasn't weird, just lucky. Well, lucky until she found out that the bills were counterfeit. She also found a dead budgie in a wastepaper basket. Definitely weird. Rosa found a pencil case full of all different flavoured and coloured condoms. That wasn't too odd, until an eighty-six-year-old lady came back to claim them.

"I once found a couple of freaky porn mags in the bathroom," said Maria. "And, I do mean freaky. There were animals and shit in there." She shuddered and drank down the rest of her tea.

"Oh, honey," remarked Justin, pausing for dramatic emphasis with his hand up in the air, "that's nothing. I once found a collection of butt plugs in a briefcase under the bed. And they all had faces painted on them." He broke down into a fit of giggles. "One was even painted up like George Bush!"

"Ewww!!" We all laughed. Except Maria. She put down her mug and asked, "What's a butt plug?"

"Okay, Miss Grenwood," the voice of the crisp receptionist cut in to Natalie's daydream in which she was checking into the Hotel St. Germain in Paris and not a three star hotel in her own city. "You're booked into Room 304. Go to the end of the lobby, catch the elevator on the left. When you get to the third floor, turn right and it will be the second door on your right." She smiled and her cute blond bob swung a bit at her chin, below which sat a neat uniform bow tied with deft, efficient fingers. Natalie stared at her for a moment. She reminded her of some green-jacketed flight attendant on the world's biggest, most garish airplane. Natalie thought the girl reminded her of a giant housefly buzzing uselessly at some corner of the window with her deft directions and brightly coloured uniform. She grabbed the key, took her receipt and mumbled a thank you, still wondering how the fuck anyone could memorize every possible route to every possible room in this entire fucking building. She could barely make it to the bathroom at night in her apartment without stubbing a toe or opening the linen closet door instead, even on those rare sober Monday and Tuesday nights.

Inside the room, she dropped her monogrammed briefcase on the top of the bureau and sighed. She ran a manicured finger over the engraved gold plate, 'Natalie R. Grenwood.' Soft tan calfskin with 24kt brass electroplate hinges and horn back crocodile detailing. Set her back $2400, but she was worth it. This bag said more about her than her resumé, more than the six years she struggled through schooling on her own, more than the miles she put between herself and the little community that threatened to hold her down. But that was all behind her now, or rather, beneath her. She had stepped on those barriers with $300 pumps and was so far up the ladder everyone else was looking up her skirt.

The room was quiet and confined, precious in a mass-produced way. It felt like she had been shoved into the velveteen-lined insides of a child's jewellery box or into a cotton ball bag. It made her feel angular and restless.

The bed was huge. It was covered in a creepy-looking spread consisting of different sized blotches in shades of metallic green.

It made her feel very single. Vengefully, she threw herself onto it headfirst like a four-year-old in a temper tantrum.

The day had been long and complicated before it deposited her here in this poorly decorated room. It was chaotic from the moment she sprinted from her bedroom, already late.

"Fuck, fuck, fuck." Natalie hopped across the living room floor with a Barbie shoe embedded in her right foot. She normally used excessive profanity only in emergency situations, but having a tiny plastic stiletto rammed into your heel is as good a reason as any to swear. Her five-year-old daughter Cleo ran by in a fairy dress and tiara, screaming, "Fuck, fuck, fuck," to the tune of 'It's a Small World After All.' A taxi honked impatiently from outside. She barely had time to chase down the fairy like some pinstriped linebacker and ram on her rubber boots. She tossed a half eaten Pop Tart into Cleo's pet bunny cage, promising to pick up nutritious vegetable-type food for it on the way home. Seat belted in and with the x-rated version of 'Small World' running at full blast, they were off to drop Cleo at the school and then to the train station. It was 7:45 a.m.

Later that morning she was sitting at her desk wondering if the Fruit Roll Up she was snacking on (forgot to take Cleo's lunch out of her purse this morning) could actually be classified as fruit, thus alleviating any guilt that might be festering its way through her stubborn cerebellum, sneakily implanted by some Kremlin-style article in Cosmo.

It had been a pretty productive day. So far, she'd bought $164 worth of really useful items off of e-Bay and managed to remember to ask the receptionist to take messages for her as she was in an important meeting. She was sure there were other things that she could be doing, but at that moment she was in a pretty vicious bidding war with some bitch from Utah, a cow-faced type who managed to hook up her computer via solar power no doubt.

What did she need with a pair of patent leather Jimmy Choo boots anyways?

Panic. Half an hour later she realized that she had spent $164 on things she would never use: a corset, a pink Swiss Army knife, a Hello Kitty alarm clock for her hideously lazy child and a pair of Ralph Lauren tweed slacks—one size too small—in anticipation of all the weight she would start losing as soon as the last of Cleo's forgotten Twinkies were finished off. She was horribly behind on the monthly report she was set to deliver at the staff meeting she herself had called for twenty minutes from now.

Natalie worked for a medium sized consulting firm that mainly produced business literature like brochures, reports, research papers and proposals for non-profits and, as her Board of Directors was fond of saying, 'issue-based' agencies. Her whole life was issue based. She had her own office and an assistant who ensured that she always had time to nip out for Thai food at odd hours of the afternoon.

Her thirtieth birthday was less than two wine-soaked, manic-depressive months away, months that would be filled with frantic calls to various friends declaring the end of glorious youth and her threatening to throw herself off the roof of her garage—until they reminded her that the short fall would perhaps only result in a sprained ankle. What supportive friends she had. Being recently reflective, Natalie couldn't shake the feeling that something was missing.

She thought perhaps her mood had to do with the fact that her only boyfriend was lying in her top drawer nestled comfortably beside the underwear she didn't fit into anymore and should really throw out because their arrogant lace depressed her. But even that was useless as she kept forgetting to buy double A batteries. Goddammit, no wonder she couldn't maintain a healthy relationship with any sort of real person. She couldn't even remember to buy her vibrator new batteries.

The staff meeting passed in a blur. Statistics. Profit margins. Proposals to write. Reports to hand in. Annoying co-workers she needed to give unnecessary assignments to. Then at two o'clock in the afternoon the Chairman of the Board called her. "Natalie, there's a conference tomorrow morning I need you to go to. It's in town, but there's a room booked for the agency over there. We were expecting Miranda from the Montreal office to fly in for it, but she can't make it. Getting her wisdom teeth out or some bullshit. Anyways, you can head over tonight if you want."

Hmmm, a night out, away from the house that bluntly reminded her that she was horrible at domestic-type stuff. A night where she could watch soft-porn by herself without having to switch to Wheel of Fortune every time her little girl wandered into the living room to ask for a glass of water, a snack, a monster room check or a blood transfusion to help her sleep. Sometimes, Natalie worried that Cleo picked up a little too much of her own sarcasm and foul language for comfort, which is probably why the other mothers never stopped to talk after playgroup.

She called her sister right away and asked her to pick up Cleo and watch her for the evening. Then she hit the mall and bought clothes for the next day so she didn't have to go home at all. Now flopped out on the bed, she decided to get settled in and maybe make a trip down to the convenience store. Natalie made her way to the 7-Eleven and bought two iced cappuccinos in square glass bottles, a big bag of white cheddar popcorn, a dark chocolate bar, two licorice whips, three glossy tabloid magazines and a pack of large Players Extra-Light Regulars. She was looking forward to a night of doing absolutely nothing of importance.

She turned on the TV and decided to watch Entertainment Tonight. On a commercial break, she thought it best to put away her new clothes for tomorrow's meeting. She didn't want to leave everything in the shopping bags on the floor and risk showing up in wrinkled pants or a creased blouse.

The dresser in her room had six laminated front panelled drawers with huge faux brass pull handles. In the top was a glossy, hardcover book that banged about the empty drawer when she opened it. At first, Natalie thought that it was the stereotypical hotel Bible. She lifted it out and noted the weight of the paper and the absence of gold lettering on the front cover, then opened it.

> *"I don't want to spend my life running until there is only the memory of dying at the moment of death. I feel like I should be doing more, career-wise and for future stability, but I cannot bear not to reach out and caress everything."*

This book was someone's journal left behind in the fray of packing up and checking out. The last quarter of the book was blank and the last page written on was dated from this month, last year. Although she knew it was horrid to read someone's diary (much like raping their inner most thoughts, really) she could not deny that the prospect of doing so fascinated her.

The book survived unmolested in this drawer for a whole year likely because of its resemblance to a Bible, thought Natalie as she retrieved it from its particle board tomb, forgetting all about her clothes for tomorrow.

Throwing aside her tabloids, Natalie got settled on the bed. Flipping through the pages she saw that the handwriting was much neater at the beginning when the book was still new. Then she read:

April 23
My grandmother taught me about integrity, though I
can't recall ever being subjected to a lecture. She was born
in 1913 to an Ojibway woman of mixed reputation and
mixed blood. She grew up determined, useful, beautiful, soft
and strong, like sweetgrass on the banks of Georgian Bay;
sweetgrass that can slice your hand if you rub the wrong
way. There are pictures of her with her high cheekbones
and long dresses, her body leaning up against barns, in
fields, holding babies, smiling widely, not caring that an
iron-filled medicine had taken her teeth early on in life.

She is a wide-shouldered and starry-eyed beauty.
She looks full moon and stone-smooth steady.

She marries a man of mixed blood and mixed reputation
and they have beautiful brown babies together. Six
of them survive. They have to drop the children off
in town as the show starts and pick them up as the
theatre lets out or they are beaten up for being 'Michif,'
'Métis,' Indians, 'red niggers,' 'across the Bay dirt.'

He makes good money guiding rich cottagers and rowdy
city fishermen in his boat, an authentic Native guide. But he
stumbles and loses himself at the bottom of a whiskey bottle.
He looks through cloudy eyes at images that slide away too
fast to grasp, images that he can smell and poke at as they
careen by. He thinks that if he pushes on the sides of the bottle
hard enough, maybe it will tip and he will be free. He thinks
that maybe he will be free from the prison of being 'authentic.'

So he pushes. He pushes hard and rocks the bottle back
and forth. He yells and he hits and the blows all land on
her. She carries the wounds on those wide shoulders while
she carries her babies, moving snakes off the path with
a stick on her way down to the well to collect water.

*The man, my mishomis, is the grandfather I saw
once as a vein-etched shrunken head perched in an
easy chair watching the Bay slowly seduce the last of
his front yard into the water. He pushes and pushes
until she gathers up the last of her babies and carries
away his world on those wide, wide shoulders.*

*Through the fear and the spent nights, a few of the babies
at her knee and breast, she sits at the wooden table with
a wooden expression knowing both he and the money
are up at the hotel; through it all she remains full moon
and stone smooth steady. She turns at the door, all her
grandmothers' spirits caught up in her eyes, moving across
her face, says, "One day you're going to need me. One
day you're going to ask for me. And I won't be there."*

*Those spirits guide my grandmother's feet to the city where
her older babies have managed to fit in and forget. Years
of days pass and she always has babies at her knee and a
wide smile leaning against bus stops, in malls, against
tall buildings, holding grandchildren on wide hips.*

*My grandmother lives with my mother and I am lucky
enough to be born into this extended family. One day
I am with her in our orange and gold living room. My
mother has gone back home with her sisters to stay with
my grandfather who is on his death-bed. My grandmother
tells me this story as she slowly dries the dishes, walking
back and forth from the kitchen. The phone rings and
she puts down the crockery pot she has been drying for
ten minutes with a thin, faded checkered dishtowel. She
answers the phone, listens for a few minutes, says 'no' and
'yes' a few times, asks polite questions and then finally
says, "You tell him I told him so." Then she hangs up.*

*"Who was that mamere?" I question, walking into the
kitchen. She picks up the same pot and starts wiping
it with the same damp and faded dishtowel.*

*"Your mother, calling from the hospital. The old man is
almost gone." Her voice is different, a single thread in a
woven chorus of grandmothers. Her ancestors are resting
on her shoulders, fingers combing through gleaming hair.*

*"But why did you say 'tell him I told you so?'" I knew that
this was the last day of my grandfather's life and that a
rebuff is an unusual last remark to make to a dying man.*

*"He needed me and he asked for me." And she sits down
in the high-backed chair in the corner of our kitchen. She
wouldn't go to hold his hand while he struggled his way
into death. She didn't make the trip north to sit in the front
pew at the reasonably well-attended funeral. After eighty
years of defining the terms of a successful mortal contract,
she simply sat down with pure, blinding integrity.*

Natalie put the book down for a moment. This was not the sex
and scandal she had anticipated, and, yes, even hoped for, and it
struck something deep in her, somewhere under her ribs.

When Natalie was fourteen, she stopped participating in family
get-togethers to avoid having to spend any real time with the 'olds'
who made up her dad's family. Those people were embarrassing
anyways, with their backwards talk and long-short mullets. I
mean, really, how many different ways could you wear hunting
gear before you were officially a hick? She had almost died when
her grandmother was staying with them for a week and her friends
came over to pick her up for the movies one night. As Natalie
bounded down the stairs in her frosted pink lip-gloss, hair pulled
back in a bright blue scrunchy, she heard her friends talking in

hushed tones inside the front door. "Oh God, no," she whispered to herself as she turned the corner, "God, no."

And sure enough, there was her grandma in her knitted sweater and matching slippers, hunched over like a crooked walking stick. She was talking with Natalie's friends. The girls stood very close together holding onto the spaghetti straps of their matching purses. Natalie was the only one without a matching purse. She could barely hold onto her popular status and the last thing she needed was this old woman ruining it for her.

"So, you kids headin' to the show then, eh?" The old woman asked, smacking her gums together as she spoke. The girls nodded, tittering to each other slightly. "Back home we ain't got no 'thee-ay-tures'. But sometimes the kids will hitch into town to see a show." The girls looked at each other, smirking softly at the small town dialect that assaulted their urban sensibilities. Natalie flew into the foyer, hustling them out the screen door as quickly as she could, slamming the door behind them.

"Hey, Nat. Is that old lady, like, your grandma or something?" Tina, easily the most popular girl in junior high, asked, tossing her highlighted blonde hair over her shoulder.

"Yeah," another asked, "Are you, like, Indian or something?"

Natalie giggled nervously, "Are you kidding? Of course not you guys. C'mon. That's just some lady my mom has over every once in a while. It's, like, a volunteer thing or something." She laughed again. She laughed until they laughed and the bus came to carry them off to the mall. Shortly thereafter her grandmother, who had been in town to see a specialist about pains in her stomach, died of cancer. Natalie wore that same bright blue scrunchy and a nagging feeling of guilt to the funeral.

She opened the book again.

April 25
I spent the day at the Friendship Centre helping out
with preparations for a Round Dance we're sponsoring.
I organized the other volunteers. It was great because I
brought the kids with me and they helped make decorations
for the feast and set up the craft tables. Well, all Baby
really did was bend up all the pipe cleaners and distract the
women with his big smile, but we had fun nevertheless.

The Dance started around 7:00 p.m. We were scheduled
to begin at six, but you know how community is no one
really showed up until almost eight, except of course for the
seniors. They sat in their plastic chairs and were gossiping
about everyone by 6:30 p.m. We had a really good turnout.
Baby wooed all the aunties in the crowd and they passed him
around. Serenity was busy bossing people at the craft table
so I even got to dance a few times. Lotsa cute out of town
Native guys showed up! Too bad I couldn't stay out and
party. I had to get the kids home so I could scrub Kool-Aid
stains off their cheeks and get them into bed on time.

But, I got to thinking, looking around at my community in their
Phat Farm shirts and Sean John jeans. It's amazing how all over
the world people are willing to go so far to claim their identity;
self-mummification over an entire lifetime, skull moulding, facial
tattoos, neck elongation, and so many of us are unwilling even
to grow out our hair or wear a ribbon shirt in public. Not that I
think we have to all dress and be a certain way, but once in a while
it would be nice just to show that respect.

April 27
Today me and Nathaniel hung out after the drum social at
the university. It's nice to be able to talk about guys with an
honest to goodness guy, even though it seems that, according
to Nathaniel, no guy is ever going to be good enough for me!

Hanging out with him, I see potential for myself. When I see him with his daughter, or when I hear him sing, it makes me want something. Something more than what I have.

Nathaniel is one of those great Nish guys who can remember what seems like a million songs for the big drum. He is a great dad, takes care of himself and hasn't let himself fall into the dreaded 'drummers physique,' a big round belly with little scrawny legs. He's funny and clever. We can spend hours sitting on picnic tables and sharing plates at dinner break laughing and talking about mutual friends, indulge in gossip and talk about outings. I especially treasure his stories about house parties and barbeques since I rarely make it out anymore. What with two small kids to look after and without a partner to help I am almost overwhelmed with responsibility. It's sad that none of my relationships worked out, but I'm still grateful for the kids I ended up with, even if I do miss partying. Nathaniel always has time and patience for my kids. He lets them crawl all over him while we chat. Sometimes they lure him away to play hide and seek for hours. I feel so blessed to have him in my life.

I worked on my outfit when I got home, mainly repairs. Some beading had come loose on the leggings and a couple jingles looked like they were ready to fall. It was really nice to be home, my babies sleeping on the floor in front of me passed out after watching a Disney movie and me just working on my dress. I took my time and enjoyed the quiet. Sometimes I feel like an old woman, my pastimes are so sedate.

Natalie dropped the book here again. This girl lived a very different life, yet there were still some similarities between them. They were both from the same nation and about the same age. She realized now that she had to go to the washroom pretty badly so she made a dash for it with the book tucked under her arm. She was hooked on this sweet, involved little life.

April 30
Well, today was pretty hard. I met Nathaniel for coffee
before he caught the Greyhound back home to the rez. He
got a job there and will be gone indefinitely. We met at the
Second Cup in town after I dropped the kids off at daycare
and school, just before my classes started. I thought he
was acting a bit weird, but assumed it was because he was
stressed as usual about leaving his little girl for so long.

It turns out, he was stressing because he was there to reveal
his feelings for me. He was like, "I've liked you as more than a
friend for a really long time, I just haven't had the courage to
tell you." I was weirded out and I felt kind of intruded upon.
Like maybe all those times I cried on his shoulder and hung
out with him with my guard down, that he was trying to
find a way to get to me. And as sweet as that could be, it still
weirded me out. It was like some stranger reading my diary.

At this point, Natalie, who was lying on the bed like a big kid doing homework, dropped the book. She felt like the bellhop had just
walked in and caught her masturbating. But soon enough, her curiosity grabbed a hold of her again and she cautiously, with a furtive
glance over to the locked room door, continued her reading.

I tried to be calm and pretended to hear him out, but really, I
wondered how the hell I was going to get out of this. I mean, I
really liked Nathaniel but not like that. I ended up saying that
I thought maybe he was just confused. That perhaps he wanted
someone like me, but not necessarily me. That we were buds.

He was pretty quiet throughout it all and ended up just
nodding with his head down before he took off early. I let him
go. I had nothing left to say after. "I love you, Nathaniel," I
said to his back as he left the coffee shop. "But not like that."

Later, on the bus to get to school, I passed by him. He was smoking a cigarette outside the Greyhound Station. I wanted to wave at him, but I knew that I no longer could. I cried a bit, into my sleeve, sniffling at the back of the bus. I felt like he was already gone. I felt like he would never be back.

Before I picked up this journal tonight, after the kids were done in the bath and all tucked into bed, I picked up a pad and pencil to write him a letter. I tried several times, but kept having to erase the words that were too stiff, too misleading, too cruel. I mean, in the coffee shop, he looked at me as though I had just run over his dog. I didn't want to throw it into reverse and back up on over the poor thing again. Eventually, I rubbed a hole in the paper and I had to throw it out.

What do I do? It's worse than never seeing him again, because I know for damn sure that I'm going to see him all summer on the pow wow trail. What do we do, pretend that we're okay? Pretend that we don't know each other? It'll be like passing by the Greyhound Station without waving every day. Dammit. I'm going to sneak a smoke out the window and head to bed.

May 15
I know it's been a while, but life has been pretty busy. Still no word from Nathaniel, though his cousin and I went out for drinks on the weekend and she says he's doing okay. Apparently, he got a sweet gig facilitating a youth program on the rez and has managed to convince his ex to let Meegwans, his little girl, stay with him up there for a few months. She thinks he might stay up there this summer. I guess I'm happy for him.

It was nice being able to go out too, though I haven't partied in a while and I got pretty drunk pretty fast. A few beers and I was dancing and flirting like old times. My mom took the

*kids for a week, since she won big in bingo. She rented a car
and came to get them and took them to my sister's house in the
States to visit. I worry a lot but I know that they'll be alright
with mom, plus my sister and her husband haven't been able
to conceive yet, so I'm sure they'll be spoiled beyond belief.*

*Beyond that one night though, I've been pretty well behaved.
I finished a pair of moccasins for my cousin Patty and went
down to the Friendship Centre for the drum social. One
of my old friends who had moved away to Saskatchewan
for some government job was in town for training, so
I got to hang out with her. She invited me out there for
their pow wow in August and I think I might go. All I
need to do is hook up a ride. I could probably leave the
kids with my mom if I don't feel like taking them all the
way out there. Serenity is dancing up a storm in her new
fancy outfit, but Saskatchewan is a long haul. We'll see.*

*Sometimes I feel very lonely here in this small city. It's a lot
more crowded and complicated than back home. All my closest
friends are scattered into the four directions. The good news
is that it means I have an excuse to pack up my regalia and go
visiting. When you're new to an area and you're pow wowing,
you've got a pretty good chance at placing and winning
some nice coin. People get bored of the regulars, and being
the new girl with a different style outfit is always a bonus.*

Natalie took a breather. She herself had never been to a pow wow.
All this talk of outfits and drums was alien to her. In her family, there
wasn't much to be proud of, she supposed. Besides her grandmother,
no one took an interest in pow wows or any other traditional stuff;
unless you wanted to count drinking a box of beer and driving dirt
roads with no license traditional activities.

Natalie couldn't remember ever really being involved in her community at all. It wasn't as though she consciously avoided it, other than trying to keep her family and her social life separate. It was more like it really wasn't all that important to her, so why bother? Through this girl's days and nights she began to develop a soft, unformed sense of homesickness but, oddly, for a place she doesn't really know. It was like a blood memory had started to spill over in her head. It was a warm, smothering sense and she kept reading the diary in hopes of understanding what she was feeling.

May 23
*I don't want to be an authority on anything. I just want
to live with that feeling you get when your heart gets
undone and floats around your body, making you feel like
you've sucked dentist's gas into your soul. It's the feeling
that a breeze is lifting the corners of the curtain that lies
between a person and complete satisfaction. It's the feeling
I get when the pow wow has shut down for the day and
the entire grounds are lost in the dark expanse. It's like
when the drummers are still under the arbor then, with
their hand drums, and the wind is threatening to blow us
all down into Georgian Bay. It's like when I feel with all
certainty that I would rather die than not be Native.*

*I met a boy—well, a man, really. His name is Trevor. We
hooked up at a community meeting at the Health Centre to
discuss new funding for bringing in Traditional Teachers to
our small urban rez. He was there representing the Native
crisis intervention program that's run through the local
hospital. I was there as part of the College's Native Council.
We started talking through his second cousin who takes some
classes with me. Four of us went out for dinner afterwards.*

We pretty much segregated ourselves from the group and spent most of the time leaning into each other and talking about kids and stuff. He has five himself, which is crazy because he's only two years older than me. I guess when you're a man and you don't have to worry about delivering these chubby little guys and then getting up seven times in one night to feed them from sore breasts, it's okay to have as many as you can. I asked him if he sees them and he told me that two of his exes are in Manitoba and the other is in town so he sees his two boys on a pretty regular basis and drives out to see the others whenever he can.

We really clicked and I ended up giving him both my number and a date for this weekend. I'm nervous because whenever I start seeing a guy, I worry about losing too much of myself too quickly. I have a tendency to do that. I obviously make bad choices since I am alone right now with two kids. Not that I regret my little angels, but at the same time, they don't exactly have great dads. Serenity's dad used to be around when she was little but now that she's turned eleven and has her own mind and personality, he doesn't really make an effort. He will occasionally call, but that's usually when he's locked up again and has nothing but time on his hands. I realize now that he was just a fling from my youth and we are too different to even really be friends. Not that we hate each other, but we are definitely not friends.

And Baby, well, his father was gone before he was even born. I tell myself that it's not a big deal because I will always be there for my son, but it still hurts. It's good to know that this new guy is involved with his kids, because really, how could I expect to start anything with anyone when he can't even take care of his own blood, especially when mine are going to be around so much. See, here I go already, wondering if he'll be okay around my children and we haven't even kissed yet!!

Natalie read, completely absorbed, only stopping to open a bag of popcorn. It was as though she was scared that at any moment this woman would show up to claim her journal and take it away with her, along with any thrilling conclusions and saucy bits. She substituted licorice for dinner and didn't even call home to check on Cleo. She read about the growing relationship between the girl and her new man. She read about the day she found out that he was still with the mother of his sons and that they even lived together. She read about the continued affair, feeling a little more comfortable now that the girl was seemingly, 'not so perfect.'

> *July 3*
> *I am constantly wavering between being overwhelmed and hating my life, thinking that it is full and eclectic, like the Christmas tree we set up in our kitchen every year. Maybe I should just pull away, like a turtle into its shell, before something heavy falls on my head. I felt euphoric on Saturday morning after Trevor and I slept together and he complimented me and hinted that he wanted to stay with me and then left nonetheless. It was humid and bright and I had no kids here to worry about and the pow wow was ahead of me. I felt great. I had all the reassurance I needed even though he was going home to her and it only lasted one day. If Nathaniel and I were still friends, this is when I would call him and talk for like three hours.*
>
> *I saw Nathaniel last week at a small traditional pow wow out east. He was holding hands with a beautiful dark skinned girl and laughing. And he looked amazing in his infatuation with his two long braids and his wide, straight smile. He caught me looking and threw a bit of that smile over to me. But unlike the American gathering last month where we ran into each other and he played with the kids for hours, they weren't with me this time, so he had no obligation to come over and hang out at all. The shine from his clean white T-shirt and his even smooth teeth stayed in my eyes all afternoon.*

July 5
I ended it today with Trevor and I feel light. He was never
mine to begin with and I feel horrible stealing away someone's
daddy, if even for one dinner or an overnight visit when
their parents are fighting. And so here I am at two in the
morning alone, in my bedroom, lit only by a string of little
white Christmas lights. Everyone else is asleep, which makes
me want to do something with these precious minutes before
sleep takes over, something profound or inspiring. Instead,
like always, thoughts of not paying the rent on time and
dealing with creditors take over. I wish I could do something
besides worry about bone-grinding financial woes.

Fuck it. I have no inspiration and unless I receive
divine intervention the next thirty seconds I'm
going to sit in my living room and smoke.

Okay, so here I am in the living room. Having a smoke.
Sitting here alone with my children in their beds and my
head spinning from worry as much as from the cigarette.
I realize how fragile my world is, how it see-saws back
and forth between stress and effort. I feel like I've built the
foundations of my life with little, uneven cubes of glass and
now the wind is starting to rage. How achingly clear it all is
at an hour which has no witnesses. I don't want to develop
analysis paralysis about my situation, but I do know that
men and their inability to stay in my life or to be anything
other than a headache have caused a lot of this stress.

I heard a great joke at lunch with my girlfriends today.
What's the difference between a Native man and a picnic
table? A picnic table can support a family. I laughed all
the way to the Money Mart where I cashed my child tax
benefit cheque so I could buy diapers and some apples.
Thank God for friends with their good humour and poor
taste otherwise I'm sure I'd be depressed right now.

July 11

I placed this weekend. I took second place in my category and picked up $800! I feel like this money is 'reward money' and that I should definitely splurge. Even better than that, I feel way more confident dancing. It felt awesome to be standing in front of so many Native people, shaking the judges' hands, collecting that little brown envelope full of folded twenties. I felt like a champion.

I'm so glad my kids were there to see. They were really proud of me and clapped and jumped up and down when I waved to them. It was amazing to sit on our stripy blanket in the shade, eating snow cones and laughing. We were a really happy little family and for a moment I felt like I didn't need anyone but them beside me for me to succeed, although there were lots of people beside me. I ran into a bunch of people I knew back in the first youth program I was a part of when I came to the city and a couple cousins who had driven out from the rez as well. Nathaniel was there but the gathering was big enough that we could pretend that we didn't see each other. So I brought Serenity to buy her beads to finish up the designs on her yoke and held Baby while he slept and drooled contentedly on my shoulder.

July 20

Life is crazy. I never, ever would have expected to be back in Trevor's bed. Well, technically, he was in my bed, since he shares his bed, along with the rest of his worldly possessions and a couple of kids, with his girlfriend. And when I woke up, hung-over and full of sore, bruised-feeling spots, I knew that I would never go out with him again. It was nice to end things with an upper hand. I was sure that we were over and I wasn't sad. I felt complete in and of myself. I felt like his presence was like a sliver at the bottom of my foot, slowing me down and making it painful to walk with confident strides. Good-bye Trevor!

Summer is half over and things keep getting better.
Slowly enough so I know it's real, but quickly enough
that sometimes I feel as if my heart would burst.

Natalie did not see the sky erase the blackness from its edges and
the dark blue of the impending day fill the spaces like grains of
sand in an hour glass. She was too absorbed. She read about trips
to cousins' weddings and camping with two small children and a
couple of friends. She learned that the girl was in college in a small
city just north of this one for nursing and that she really wanted
to switch over to anthropology and archaeology at the university
here, taking her interest in all things medical with her. The girl
hoped one day to be a forensic archaeologist and to specialize in
early Native American civilizations. She figured if someone had to
learn about the past through the unearthing and preserving of her
people's remains, it may as well be her, so that she could ensure
that things were done in a respectful way. The only indication that
Nat was sleepy was her burning eyes.

There was something else about this woman's life that was addic-
tive for Natalie. Every trip she made to the washroom, the book
went with her. When she finally realized that the TV was still
on and her favourite crime show was starting, she stood up and
turned it off. It was as if she were figuring out which shape fit into
which hole in her own life. It was as if this simple book full of
mundane domestic details and barbed and luscious insights were
the very key to her life. She felt as though she had stumbled upon
the Native Rosetta Stone.

August 6
I spent the day at the school library looking up courses and
calendars. Turns out that the university down south in the
big city has exactly what I need to study archaeology. They
even have a secured partnership between the school and the
museum, giving students access to all their storerooms and

curatorial research. I sent off a few emails requesting more information and since I plan on attending the national pow wow down there in November, maybe I can take an extra day or two to meet with people and check it out. Now, if only some of the people I tried to get in touch with today would get back to me in time and so I can book meetings. I wouldn't mind moving down there if it meant I could speed up the process towards getting the degree I want.

I got an email from Nathaniel. It didn't say much, only that he was doing well in his job and that he was a bit worried and depressed because his little girl was moving to the big city in a couple months with her mom. Apparently, Meegwans' mom got a job working at a women's shelter there and was taking her along. She said he could still see his daughter whenever he could make it down or arrange for transportation for her to get up there. He was thinking about maybe just saying 'fuck it' and moving down there himself. (Which is kind of crazy since I myself was just mulling over the opportunities that may take me there!) With over thirty Native organizations in operation, there are plenty of jobs he could get there with his qualifications. Plus he speaks his language fluently.

He wasn't quite himself, but it was the closest we've been to having civilized communication since April. It would be great if we were friends still. Then we could both move to the city and be roomies. But no. Goddammit. He had to go and ruin it all that day in the coffee shop.

"Argh! This is so frustrating," Natalie muttered through gritted teeth, leaning up against the headboard, smoking her Players Extra Lights. "Hi! Wake up! Made for each other!!" She ashed her smoke into an empty iced cappuccino bottle.

Anyways, I sent a message back. It was something like this:

Hi Nathaniel,
I'm glad to hear from you ... really glad. It's been way too
long and I feel like an orphan without you. I heard from your
cousin that things are going really well for you and your
youth programming. Multi-year funding is hard to find so
you must be doing great work to secure it! Anyways, that
sucks about Meegwans and I know it might feel like the world
is crashing down, but the city isn't really a bad place for
kids. There's so much to do there and so many opportunities
for them to take advantage of as they get older. In Chinese,
the word for crisis is the same as the word for opportunity.

I've seen you a bit this summer on the trail. I see your drum
group's doing pretty well now that Cubby is sober and back
with his old lady and, of course, since you're back, are you
guys making it down to the big city pow wow this year?
I'll be there. I'm not sure if I'll be dancing. I don't know
if I have the courage to compete with hundreds of other
jingle dress dancers, but I want to go to the city anyway
to check out stuff for school. I think it's time I considered
those changes I've been talking about for so long.

I miss you and I hope we can stay up all night
talking and make each other shoot milk and cereal
out of our noses laughing again soon.
Take care.

That was it. Nothing too committal. Nothing too long or
really poetic. Just a bit of hope packaged up and arcing
its way through cyber space like a shooting star carrying
my wish for our friendship. We'll see, I suppose.

August 18
I got a response from Nathaniel. All it said was:

T:
Don't feel intimidated by other dancers. You are a champion.
But I guess you already know that's how I feel. Thanks.
N

And even though I was a bit flustered, and even though I
think that our friendship is way too important—especially
now that it has the potential to return to what it used
to be—and has no room for any outside or extra emotion
like jealousy or confusion, I wondered if he still had that
pretty dark-skinned girl holding his hand, and something
long and green clutched at my heart. And now that I
am home and reflective, I'm worried that his absence has
made me feel differently. Worried for several reasons,
but mostly because I can't afford to lose him again.

Sept 5
Serenity is back in school and surprisingly pleased about it. I
think she was starting to get bored and now that she's in grade
five and into Beyoncé. Hope she doesn't get into boys too soon.
Yipes! There's way more going on, like field trips and such. I
am also back at school, and, of course, working every available
shift at the bookstore. Trevor tried coming back into my life
talking about 'getting rid of' his girlfriend and becoming
serious but I in no way want any part of a man who can even
say things like he'll ditch his wife for another girl. It's not a
very impressive relationship resumé tactic if you ask me.

I need to be moved. Temples and fasting moved. Revelations
and stolen adventures moved. Where can I find this
movement? There is no movement in love, I think, only
movement into it, and even then, it's not honest movement,

it's falling, falling in love. After that, everything is swaddled and secure, strapped into a committed cradleboard. Muscles atrophy. Which is why any movement thereafter is fraught with monumental resistance. Stay put! I am like a fish that will suffocate in its own environment if it stops moving.

We did get funding to bring in teachers and Elders from all across the country and it's been amazing. The other day I managed to fit in an appointment with an energy therapist. I laid down on a cot that resembled a hospital bed after her helper had marked down a few details like my birthday and my nation on a sheet of paper. She hung a crystal suspended from a piece of thin rope over my supine body and it swung in little, tight circles. Every once and a while it would bounce from side to side and she would say, "Hmmm," or, "Ahhh," and her helper would scribble incoherent looking lines on her clipboard.

I closed my eyes in the dimness of that room and I heard her small voice boom large from somewhere near my feet. "I see you conducting a great orchestra, but the musicians aren't playing instruments. They are settling the air around a large group of people. They are making the air breathable and you are allowing them to do so." And before I could even think to ask a question, I heard her again from near my right elbow.

"You are standing before a column of light that has always been there. You are reaching into the column, and, even though it seems like there is nothing there, that you can clearly see the other side of the room through this blue, murky light, you are still pulling out objects. The first object is a feather dressed in red beads with tan hide. The second is a book filled with hieroglyphics that I can't quite make out. The third is a blue cloth pouch tied with a yellow string. This makes you smile as you hold it. You loop the yellow string around your

neck and carry the pouch against your heart as though it carries substance of great importance. The last is a rock, a round grandfather worn smooth by waves and years. You are learning what to do with these tools. And eventually you will.

She said lots of other stuff about balancing all my mental, physical, emotional and spiritual sides. She said she had realigned everything that was out of whack and I wasn't quite sure if I felt more balanced when I left, but I certainly felt more relaxed and intrigued. A feather, a hieroglyphs book, a pouch and a grandfather rock. What could it all mean? All I could figure out was that at least I was picking up tools along my journey and that eventually I would know what to do with them in order to help my community live with bigger, fuller breaths. That made me feel pretty good about myself.

Natalie didn't notice that the street below her had begun to come alive. Her curtains weren't shut, but her eyes were, to everything but these pages. Her ears were closed to everything but this girl's voice, so clearly singing from these paragraphs and days. She looked forward to what each day might bring for her and her growing children. She knew each of her aunties by the stories that were told about them, even though their names were rarely mentioned. She cried when the baby's dad came to see him and the boy didn't recognize him. She laughed when the girl accidentally mooned her Infectious Diseases class when the partition that was blocking her as she changed into a hospital gown for a diagnostic skit fell with a great clamber to the ground. The day came over this hotel and stuck its toes into the room, but went unnoticed.

October 19
Well, I saw Nathaniel's finally. He was in town helping 'the ex' pack up for her big move to the city. I knew he would be down around the end of the month, but I wasn't sure what day. I've been thinking about him a lot so when he showed

up on my doorstep last night, I was a little nervous. I mean, it has been six months since our friendship dissolved in a cup of coffee and at least three since I'd laid eyes on him.

'Hey N," I smiled through lowered eyelashes, locked together like a Chinese puzzle.

"What's up T," he responded. He didn't wait for an invitation to come in. Baby was off with his paternal grandparents for the weekend and Serenity was at a big girl sleepover. I had actually just been finishing off new leggings. I decided to incorporate my spirit name into the design and I was sewing black cut glass beads into the owl's eyes so they would shine. He inspected my work and then flopped down on the couch.

It's weird when you are in a relationship that is suddenly changing. It's like that wooden toy where the thin blocks are held together with fabric ribbons in confusing ways that allow them to tumble down over each other and make pleasant clicking noises as they do. It's like everything is changing in a way where you don't really notice, in a way where everything is really the same, but completely new. I felt the tumbling deep in my belly.

We talked for a bit and he told me that while he was here helping the ex pack, they were actually sharing the moving van. He decided that he wanted to be closer to Meegwans and was going ahead and transporting his life to the city. At first, I was worried. Yes, I admit it, I was worried that they were sharing more than the van, but he told me about how he would be staying with his cousin until he could find his own place and how he already had two interviews lined up for youth programming in the city. Apparently, his funder on the reserve had made a few calls for him.

*I told him that I would be around next month. I had already
scheduled a meeting at the University to talk to the Dean for
the school I was hoping to study with if given the chance.
He seemed happy and I remembered how handsome he
could be with that big flashy smile and sharp cheekbones.*

*And then in an innocent tussle over the remote (we were
watching a DVD of the last competition pow wow where
Nathaniel's drum took first and Serenity danced real hard
and was 'caught on tape') I ended up on his lap, facing
him, my lower half completely pressed against his. I felt
everything in such exquisite detail but didn't stop play
fighting in case he moved away or I had to get up so that
we didn't get freaked out. I could definitely tell that he
could feel everything in the same way, because now he was
hard. And in a state beyond all craziness, I wasn't mad, or
scared, or grossed out, or even willing to get off his lap!*

*Then, of course, the ex called and said that she
and Meegwans were ready and he had to go. We
hugged goodbye and then he was gone.*

Fuck.

"Fuck," Natalie hissed in agreement and shared frustration, lips
clenched around yet another cigarette. "Fucking ex." She was
close to the end of the book and she felt that creeping sense of
disappointment one feels when heavily involved with characters
that are about to have the plug pulled on them. She felt on the
verge of abandonment.

Natalie couldn't walk away from T. now. She was too close. She knew
that the woman hated the way her hips were just a little too soft at
the top. "Me too," she whispered out loud. She knew that T. woke
up late some mornings and inadvertently swore at her children only

to kiss that soft spot at the very tops of their heads, the spot that smells like spices and flowers on all children, hoping to make that harshness melt away from their day. "Oh my God, I love that spot," Natalie agreed, nodding her head.

But perhaps beyond the familiarity of single motherhood and complicated relationships that made one want to scream and tear at one's hair in a very unattractive and slightly lunatic ways, there was the foreignness of a life so close to her own. Memories that were not her own sailed on blood and water and settled into her cells. Something was missing and it had nothing to do with her mechanical, yet faithfully obedient boyfriend sitting in the bottom of the nightstand drawer back home in her bedroom. And now, finally, she knew what it was. It was this, it was T. Her life, her thoughts, her community, the constant embrace she found herself in no matter what was happening across the pages of her days made her want to live differently. She didn't want to read the last few pages, but she couldn't really stop herself, much in the same way she couldn't stop lighting the last cigarette just now.

November 18
Well, I made it to the Big City. I've just checked into my hotel room. It's nice, pretty basic, but close to downtown. I love the sounds of busy, full lives spinning and colliding all around me. It's kind of a reaction to the quiet of my childhood I think. Anyways, I called Nathaniel and left a message on his cell phone. Hopefully he calls back soon.

Yay! My regalia's all ready to go. I finally got those hair ties from Patty that she's been promising to me since I finished her moccasins. I still haven't decided if I'm going to dance or not, but at least I know I can if I want to. It's kind of how I feel about Nathaniel. What if I fall, or do terribly? What if I am so embarrassed and disappointed that I stop enjoying dancing altogether? I couldn't live with that. But then again, what if I do really well and then I have something that I can carry with me for the rest of my life in a beautiful little pouch somewhere in amongst my memories? Something that I can open up later on and smell and touch and feel all over again? I don't want to pass up that chance. I couldn't live with that either.

Yippee! Nathaniel just called. He's coming by to get me and we're heading out to grab some breakfast before Grand Entry. I'm all full of butterflies, like fancy dancers are twisting their way through my ribcage. Wish me luck!

And that was it. Natalie stared at that last sentence for a full minute before she lowered the book and exhaled her last plume of smoke. She stubbed out the butt end of her cigarette and turned her head towards the window. It was the first time she noticed that it was daytime, sharp and firm.

"Oh, shit," she drawled. The clock said it was 8:43 a.m. She had seventeen minutes to get showered and dressed and to somehow mainline enough coffee to make it through the opening remarks for the meeting where she was scheduled to be. She had forgotten the reason she was in this hotel in the first place. Lethargy pulsed in her temples along with the beginnings of a wicked junk food and smoke-a-thon migraine.

Natalie jumped in to the spotless, ceramic shower with its shiny tiles and individually packaged shampoo and conditioner bottles. Her skin was sallow and grimy with smoke and grease. She stayed in for as long as she could without panicking over the time and leapt out of the bathroom like a naked gazelle. She threw on her new blouse that had been creased and pushed off the edge of the bed. She threw on wrinkled pants and a decent pair of shoes. With her hair still wet, lipstick put on like a five-year-old girl digging through her nana's handbag and slightly crumpled clothes, she was not a picture of professionalism or even of guaranteed sanity.

But it was better, she agreed, than the time she had misread her calendar book and shown up for the Governor General's luncheon in a bright red Bob Marley T-shirt. (*"Yes, your Honour, we are taking great steps as a community towards both prevention and intervention,"* she might as well have said. *"And would Your Honour like to come out back and have some tokes off a big fatty?"*)

She opened the front door and saw today's newspaper, thoughtfully placed there by sweet-faced hotel staff like helpful little mice or slightly creepy shoe elves of some sort. She picked it up and dashed down the hall. In the elevator she glanced down at the front page. The picture there was hard to miss with all its colour and movement. It was a close up of a young girl twirling about in a fancy dress. Her shawl was extended like the shiny, turquoise wings of a glassed and exhibited specimen, her face blurred by motion and determination. The caption below her read, "Twelve-year-old Serenity Johnson dances in the first day of the city's three day pow wow. The festivities begin again today at noon."

Natalie felt trapped in a surreal moment, the universe folding in up on itself like a Jacob's Ladder. This couldn't be the same girl, and yet here she was, one leg raised in mid air, hair braided up and fastened with beaded clips and ribbon ties. This was the girl she felt she knew so well though this was the first time she saw her beautiful brown skin or her huge determined eyes. The girl she knew so well through her mother's writings. Oddly, Natalie felt a surge of pride.

She got off the elevator and passed the front reception. She walked past the registration desk and through the revolving doors (she always had to fight the urge to stay in these doors and to turn around and around in it like a small child or a cartoon character). She had to find the end to the book, she had to know about the grand and beautiful conclusions.

In the cab she tucked the journal into her $2400 bag. She was going to try to find T. and return the book to her. She hoped they could talk, but, if not, it would be enough to put a face to the biography. And somewhere in the crowds, she was hoping to find that warm comfort that skated across the journal pages.

Pulling up to the stadium, she felt queasy. She handed ten dollars to the driver and opened the door. She was nervous and short of breath, like fancy dancers were twisting their way through her ribcage.